Dancing at the Odinochka

Also by Kirkpatrick Hill

The Year of Miss Agnes
Winter Camp
Toughboy and Sister

MARGARET K. MCELDERRY BOOKS

Dancing at the Odinochka

KIRKPATRICK HILL

Margaret K. McElderry Books

New York   London   Toronto   Sydney

Margaret K. McElderry Books
An imprint of Simon & Schuster
Children's Publishing Division
1230 Avenue of the Americas
New York, New York 10020

OCT 0 3 2005

This book is a work of fiction. Any references to historical events, real people, or real locales are used fictitiously. Other names, characters, places, and incidents are products of the author's imagination, and any resemblance to actual events or locales or persons, living or dead, is entirely coincidental.

Book design by Ann Zeak
The text for this book is set in Kaatskill.
Manufactured in the United States of America

10 9 8 7 6 5 4 3 2 1
Library of Congress Cataloging-in-Publication Data
Hill, Kirkpatrick.
Dancing at the Odinochka / Kirkpatrick Hill.—1st ed.
p. cm.
Summary: In the 1860s, Erinia Pavaloff's life at a trading post in Russian America gets more complicated when the United States purchases the region and members of the small community become American Alaskans.
ISBN 0-689-87388-3 (hardcover)
[1. Russians—Alaska—History—Fiction. 2. Trading posts—Fiction. 3. Alaska—History—To 1867—Fiction. 4. Alaska—Annexation to the United States—Fiction.] I. Title.
PZ7.H55285Dan 2005
[Fic]—dc22
2004003356

FIRST
EDITION

This book is for two of Erinia's many-times-removed nieces—my sister, Johanna Harper, who sent me Erinia's memoir, and my daughter, Kiki, who was the model for Erinia. And for Arnold Griese, who wrote the first Alaskan historical fiction for children.

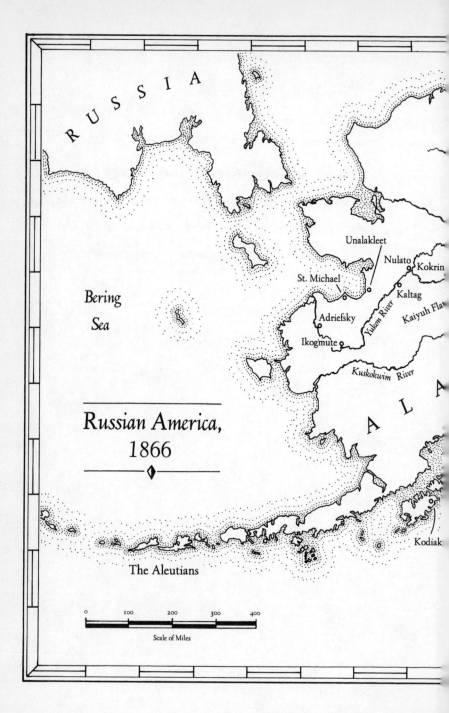

RUSSIA

Bering

Sea

Unalakleet

Nulato Kokrin

St. Michael Kaltag

Kaiyuh Fla

Adriefsky Yukon River

Ikogmute

Kuskokwim River

Russian America,
1866

ALA

Kodiak

The Aleutians

0   100   200   300   400

Scale of Miles

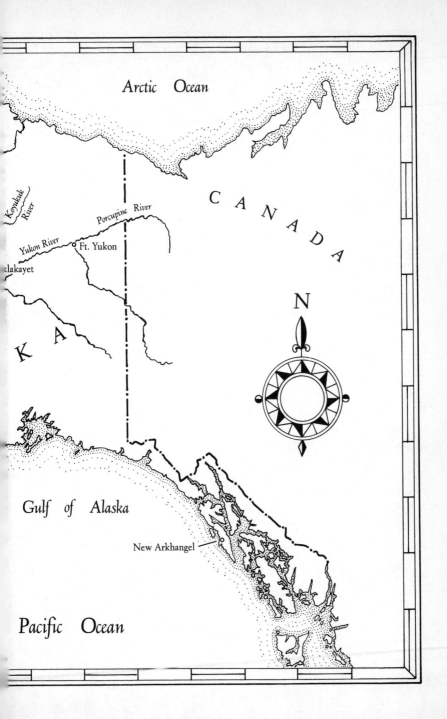

Arctic Ocean

CANADA

Koyukuk River

Porcupine River

Yukon River   Ft. Yukon

clakayet

K A

N

Gulf of Alaska

New Arkhangel

Pacific Ocean

Dancing at the Odinochka

PART ONE

The Old Days

Chapter One

NEARLY 150 YEARS AGO, WHEN ALASKA BELONGED TO Russia and was called Russian America, a little girl named Erinia Pavaloff lived with her family at the Nulato odinochka, on the banks of the Yukon River.

An *odinochka* was a trading post, a place for the native people to trade their furs. The odinochkas belonged to the Russian American Company, which wanted all the furs they could get to send back to Russia. The Indians and Eskimos wanted the things the Russians had to trade, especially tobacco and tea.

Not very many people lived in Russian America. Papa said it was a huge, empty country, not like the rest of the world, which was full of villages and towns and cities.

There weren't even any villages along the Yukon, just a few Russian forts and odinochkas close to the mouth of the river. Papa said in all of Russian America there were only a few very small towns, and those were far, far away from Nulato.

He said that if Erinia were a bird and could fly up over the odinochka, she would see thousands of spruce trees and birches and cottonwoods stretching in all directions. And across the wide Yukon she'd see the flats, tundra with countless grass lakes and winding creeks glittering in the sun. And maybe in all that wilderness, maybe up the Koyukuk River above them, she might see a bit of smoke from an Indian camp, but that would be all.

Thinking about all that emptiness didn't make Erinia feel lonesome. Erinia never felt lonesome, because everyone at the odinochka took care to see that she was happy. Mamma said they spoiled her.

Besides Erinia and Papa and Mamma, seven other people lived at the Nulato odinochka. Mamma was Athabascan, and Lena Kozevnikoff was Aleut, but the rest were creoles. That was what the Russians called native people who had Russian fathers or grandfathers.

Old Man Kozevnikoff and Lena had a grown-up boy, Elia, and there were also Erinia's big brothers, Minook and Pitka, and the workers, Stepan and Mikhail. That made ten altogether.

Erinia's big sister used to live there too, and then it was eleven. Her real name was Ekaterina, but they never called her that because it was too long to say. They called her Kate.

She was very good and quiet, like Mamma, so Erinia didn't miss her too much.

Kate was at Ikogmute, way downriver. There was an odinochka there and a mission as well. The priest took a few children like Kate to teach there.

Papa said perhaps Erinia would go there when she was older, but Erinia knew when that time came, she'd just make such a fuss that Papa would change his mind. She was never going to leave Nulato.

The odinochka was made of logs and was built around three sides of a large, square yard. Erinia could run from one end of the building to the other without ever going outdoors.

The windows were all in the front, looking out on the yard. Papa said there were no windows in the back so that only the front of the building needed defending in case of raids.

At opposite ends of the building stood two tall, square watchtowers, so people could climb up and look all around to see if danger was coming. Erinia was not allowed to go up into the towers because the stairs were so steep. She did go up sometimes, though, when no one was looking. She liked the way things looked from up there, smaller and squattier.

All around the odinochka there was a tall, tall fence with a big gate. The fence and gate were made of spruce poles fitted tightly together, and the tops of the poles were cut into sharp points.

Papa told Erinia that every odinochka in Russian America had a tall fence like that because of raids.

When Erinia wanted to know why there were raids, Papa and Old Man Kozevnikoff said it was because after the Russians came into the country, people started to get diseases they'd never had before, and they blamed that sickness on the Russians. And because sometimes they thought the Russians cheated them when they were trading.

But they said that most of the trouble was because the Russians interfered with the trading that had gone on before they came. Those Indian and Eskimo bands who had been the biggest traders were not happy to lose business to the Russians.

Mamma didn't like to have the men talking about such things to Erinia, so she'd tell them sharply, *"Daalek,"* be quiet, or she'd hustle Erinia out of the room.

There were wars between the native people as well as attacks on the Russians. When Mamma was a young woman, there had been a terrible attack on Nulato. The

Koyukuk people killed more than a hundred of Mamma's people. They stuffed up the entrances to their underground houses with burning canoes so the people inside would die from the smoke. The ones who got out of the houses, choking with smoke, they killed with arrows.

Then they ran down to the odinochka and killed Mamma's first husband, who was the Russian in charge. He was sick, but the raiders burst into the room and killed him in his bed while Mamma bravely tried to protect him. He was buried in the Russian cemetery at the top of the hill, and sometimes Minook and Pitka took Erinia there to look at the grave.

Erinia felt sorry for Mamma's first husband, to have died so horribly, but mostly she felt sorry for Mamma, who'd seen such a terrible thing. She wondered if that was why Mamma so seldom smiled and almost never laughed. Mamma worried all the time.

Erinia never worried, but she might have if she had known that one day she would have to be as brave as Mamma had been.

Erinia's family lived on one of the three sides of the odinochka, the middle part was the store, and in the other side were the barracks, where Stepan and Mikhail and the boys lived. Next to the barracks were two big rooms for the Kozevnikoffs.

Behind the store building was a little bathhouse and two small log houses where tools and oil for the petroleum lamps were stored. And that was all of the odinochka.

There were no Eskimo people near Nulato, only Athabascan Indians, Mamma's people. The Indian families who came to trade didn't live in one place like most of the Eskimos did. They moved every season to a different spot: winter camp when it snowed, fishing camp in summer, muskrat camp in the spring, fall camp in the autumn. Erinia thought it must be exciting to be moving all the time, to see so much of the world, and she always felt a little jealous when she stood on the riverbank and watched the Indians go off to a new place.

But she liked her home very much too.

Old Man Kozevnikoff was the *baidarshchik*, the person in charge of the odinochka. He spoiled Erinia more than anyone. He called her Erinochka and cut pieces for her from the loaf of sugar.

He was a lot older than Papa and had white, white hair that stood out all around his head, and a bushy white mustache.

Every week he would shave with a long, sharp razor that he sharpened on a leather strap that hung on a nail by the washbasin. Then he'd take the little paper-framed mirror from its hook on the wall and peer into it, pulling his mouth sideways, turning his face this way and that to see if he'd missed anything.

It was the only mirror in the odinochka, so when he finished and was drying his face on his shirt, he'd let Erinia look into it. She'd carefully examine one brown eye at a time, run her finger over her eyebrows to smooth them down, and open her mouth to examine her teeth.

Once she'd been shocked to see her tonsils quivering in the back of her throat like something alive, and she'd let out a yell.

Kozevnikoff laughed so hard at that he had a coughing fit and his Lena had to pound on his back for a long time.

Lena told Erinia stories whenever she wanted them. Lena was born in the Aleutian Islands, far away from Nulato, so her stories were about seals and whales, animals Erinia had never seen, but that didn't matter. They were wonderful stories, and Lena told them with great swoops of her fat arms and with a different voice for each animal. No one told stories as well as Lena.

Elia, the Kozevnikoffs' son, was a tall, handsome boy who was the best hunter at the odinochka, and Erinia had liked him so much when she was a baby that she had learned to say his name even before she learned to say Mamma or Papa. Elia liked to tease her about that.

Pitka and Minook teased her, of course, but they spoiled her too. They let her do almost everything with them, even though she was a girl. When they were taking the dog team to the water hole, they'd put Erinia to ride in the sled basket, and in the summer they'd take her in the canoe down to the sandbar to get driftwood. But of course they wouldn't let her go if there was any danger, like open places in the ice where the rushing black water showed through or whitecaps in the river.

Her brothers were just a year apart in age, but the year that Erinia was six Pitka's voice slowly changed over the summer and became deep and rumbling. It was such a funny voice to be coming out of skinny, long-legged Pitka that sometimes Erinia had to laugh at him.

And the next year Minook's voice started to do the same thing, but it couldn't make up its mind how it would sound yet, so sometimes he squeaked and croaked when he started to speak. Papa said that happened to all boys.

"Does it happen to girls, too?" Erinia asked.

"No," said Papa.

"Why not?"

Papa made a face and didn't answer. Erinia could tell he was thinking. "I don't know," he said at last. At least once a day Erinia asked questions that Papa had to answer like that.

Stepan, the oldest of the workers, was always making something for Erinia. When she was younger, he had carved her clever wooden toys with parts that moved: a dog whose head turned from side to side, a little man that could dance on a stick. When she was five, he had made her a wonderful little birch-wood bow with some bone-tipped arrows.

Stepan's left eye was covered with a blue film. When he was very little, he'd been standing too close when his father was chopping wood and a chip had flown into his eye. So that eye was blind now. Stepan wouldn't let Erinia come into the wood yard while they were chopping, in case it should happen to her.

Mikhail, the other worker, taught Erinia to use the bow Stepan had made and was very patient with her. He had a lame foot, which he was born with and which gave him a funny side-to-side way of walking, but he walked just as fast as everyone else.

Old Man Kozevnikoff never stopped teasing Stepan and Mikhail about having no wives, and whenever they went on a trading trip to Unalakleet or to Saint Michael, he told them that they must bring back a wife. But they never did. Erinia thought that was because they were very happy as they were, two old bachelors smoking their pipes together at night. Erinia was glad for that. She liked things to stay the same.

Chapter Two

THE WINTER MONTHS ON THE YUKON WERE LONG AND dark and very cold. The smoke from the stoves went straight up and hung there, suspended, over the odinochka. In the few hours of daylight the sky was pink from the little bit of sun peeking over the hill, and the trees were pink too and heavy with thick frost.

In the winter everyone at the odinochka worked hard from first light until it grew too dark to see. There was wood to chop for the stoves and water for cooking and cleaning to get. Sometimes they gathered buckets of snow to melt in the kitchen water barrel, and sometimes they dipped water from the hole chopped in the river. Snares had to be set, and someone had to put the fish trap under the ice and check it every day. The dogs had to be fed, the tools had to be fixed and sharpened, and there was work to do in the store.

Mamma and Lena cooked and cleaned, and washed the clothes and linen, but their most important job was sewing. And Erinia had to sit with them every day to learn.

Every woman had a sewing kit, which was rolled up and tied when it wasn't being used. When it was unrolled, it could be hung on the wall next to you so everything was handy.

Mamma would send Erinia to get her sewing kit and bring it to the kitchen table, where she and Lena were working by the oil lamp. Mamma had made a lovely sewing kit for Erinia out of soft smoked moose hide, and the edge of each pocket was trimmed with bright calico scraps.

A sewing kit had to have an awl for punching holes. The sharp steel needles were good for thin skins, like rabbit or marten, but were hard to push through thick ones, like moose. If the skin was thick, you had to punch a hole with the awl and push the sinew thread through the hole.

A piece of tough moose hide was used to protect your fingers from the sharp needle. It helped, but not a lot. Mamma's fingers were so rough with needle scars that her fingers snagged in Erinia's hair when she was braiding it.

A little *tlaabaas*, a curved knife, was used to cut the skins, but Erinia wasn't allowed to do that yet. She was still too young and might ruin a skin.

There was also dried sinew in the sewing kit. When you got ready to sew, you twisted the pieces of sinew together to make a long thread. But not too long. Too long was a lazy man's thread. If you wanted a long thread so you wouldn't have to thread so many needles, that meant you were lazy.

Erinia always made her thread too long.

She was glad that she was learning, but she didn't really like to sew, mostly because she had to sit down to do it. Before long she'd be wriggling in her chair, scrunching down to stretch her feet out, dropping her needles, and being careless.

Mamma's face would grow stern. "A woman who can't sew is useless," she would say.

Erinia didn't want to be useless.

Every animal the men got when they went hunting, and every bird or rabbit Mamma snared, was carefully skinned. And then Mamma and Lena would tan that skin and put it away in the fur room of the store.

There were caribou and muskrat skins tanned for parkas, rabbit skins for blankets and socks, beaver skins for mittens, caribou fawn skins to make lovely soft gloves, feathers for decoration, and fish skins for making bags and boots. Even the little pieces of leftover fur they saved for fancy trims.

There was so much sewing to do: pants and parkas and winter boots, summer moccasins, waterproof boots, gloves and mittens and summer shirts. There was no end to it. Mamma never said, "There. We're finished and we don't have to sew for a week or a month." Erinia had to learn to sew as well as Mamma because Mamma said, "Someday my eyes will go bad, and then you must do it all yourself."

Erinia would look hard at Mamma's dark eyes to see if they were going bad yet. There were more and more deep lines around Mamma's eyes, but her eyes themselves looked just the same. Erinia was glad about that because she hardly knew how to sew anything yet.

Erinia was always relieved when the sewing time was over and it was time to help with other chores.

Erinia was very helpful.

When the boys were working in the wood yard, she'd struggle into the house with big baskets loaded with birch bark and moss and shavings for fire starter.

While Mamma made a spark with a flint to start the fire, Erinia would blow vigorously on the shavings, though sometimes she blew so hard that she blew out the tiny flame and Mamma had to start over.

She'd bring in buckets of snow for the water barrel, but

she was too short to reach the top of the barrel without help, so a lot of the snow ended up on the floor.

Erinia was so busy and so quick, dashing here and there to help with this and that, that she almost wore Mamma out cleaning up the mess.

So when Mamma thought Erinia had helped her enough, she'd send her to the store. "See if Papa and Old Man Kozevnikoff need any help."

Erinia's house had real mica windows Papa had gotten from the company at Saint Michael when she was a baby. Mamma loved those windows so much she polished them every day with a soft rabbit skin.

The windows in the store were just greased seal intestines, which let in some light, but you couldn't see anything out of them.

The store was wonderful, though, even if it didn't have mica windows.

On a long table by the windows was the shiny copper samovar Papa had brought with him when he came north from New Arkhangel. You made tea with a samovar, strong, hot tea. You had to hold a piece of sugar in your teeth while you drank the tea.

That was very hard to do, and Erinia couldn't do it yet.

Right in the middle of the store there was the big woodstove made of gray stone, and by the door was a pile of wood taller than Erinia. Papa and Old Man Kozevnikoff said they were always glad to have Erinia help them. She'd take the spruce boughs they used for a broom to sweep up the bits of bark and wood that fell on the floor every time they stoked the fire.

Twice a week Papa would clear all the wood out of the stove so Mamma could bake bread in the ashes. It was a big stove and could hold twenty loaves of black Russian bread. And even though that was a lot of bread, they would always run out before the next baking.

When Papa and Old Man Kozevnikoff were busy with their accounts or their orders, there were still many interesting things for Erinia to do in the store.

A big room off to the side of the display shelves was the place the furs were stored. The door was always kept shut so the furs would stay cool, but sometimes Erinia would creep in there and play.

After beaver season in the spring the room would be full of stacks of beaver pelts.

Beaver skins were stretched into round circles, and Papa stacked them on top of one another. The skin sides were as stiff as drum tops, but the fur sides were sleek and shiny and slippery. As soon as Erinia climbed to the top of the stack, the beaver pelts would begin to slide and she would have a wonderful ride until she hit the floor with a thump.

Papa would hear the noise and drag her out by her

apron strings. "Erinia, *ty zanida!*" That meant that she was a great nuisance.

Erinia also loved the little room where the special trade goods were stored.

When Papa and Old Man Kozevnikoff were making a trade, they'd throw in some little things to make their offer more interesting, things that didn't cost very much but that everyone wanted. Like buttons.

The Indians didn't use buttons in the usual way. They sewed them on their clothes for decorations, down the side seams of the pants or all over the shoulders.

Erinia loved to play with the buttons. She'd line them up in rows according to their colors and then according to their size. She'd make families out of them, with papa buttons and mamma buttons and baby buttons. There was no end to the fun you could have with buttons, and Erinia was always sorry in the spring when the buttons had all been traded away.

Besides the buttons there were packets of steel needles, which were much better than the bone needles the Indian women used to sew with. There were dozens of combs, which Papa said were made out of tortoiseshell, little tin pipes to make music on, and beads.

Erinia wasn't supposed to play with the beads because once she'd spilled a whole box of the long blue ones everyone liked so much. A lot of them had fallen down in the cracks between the floorboards, so they'd never gotten those back.

There were red and white and black beads too. And dentalium shells.

"These shells," Papa had told her, "came from far away, islands even farther south than New Arkhangel, where I was born. Little animals lived in these shells, in the ocean, and then the shells were washed up on the beach, where people found them." Erinia stared at the shells, imagining tiny animals like foxes and bears in the shells. Then she asked, "What's an ocean, Papa?"

Papa held his hands far apart. "An ocean is bigger than the Yukon River. Bigger than a thousand Yukon Rivers!"

A thousand Yukon Rivers. How could that be? Erinia frowned at Papa. He must be making fun of her.

With the trade goods there were also little brass bells, which people took for their children to play with or to tie on their dog harnesses. Erinia liked the sound the bells made, but she had to ring them very softly, one at a time, because the time she'd tied them all together on a cord, Papa had said the noise gave him a headache.

There were iron and copper bracelets and rings, which Erinia loved to try on, but best of all were the earrings: bronze earrings and earrings with glass pendants, glass with twisting colors inside of it. Those earrings were beautiful.

Every time the company sent a new supply of earrings,

Erinia would beg to put holes in her ears so she could wear earrings like Mamma and Lena and the Indian women, but Mamma always said, "Wait till you're older."

Papa said the Eskimo men at the mouth of the river had two holes cut under their lips and in those holes they wore fancy ivory ornaments. Erinia wished she could see that. Some Eskimos and Indians had holes made in their nose cartilage to hang beads on, as well as the holes under their lips, but Erinia didn't have any holes at all.

She wouldn't have holes in her nose or under her lip because Papa wouldn't stand for that, but someday she could have holes for earrings.

She could hardly wait.

When Erinia went with Mamma to set rabbit snares and ptarmigan snares, the snow, dry with cold, crunched beneath her snowshoes, and the northern lights shifted and slid over the flats in cold white sheets.

She didn't mind the cold because she loved to be outdoors and because she had such good, warm clothes.

Mamma had made her a warm muskrat parka and caribou-skin pants with the fur turned inside. Her boots were part of the pants so no snow could get down inside and freeze her feet, and every day Erinia had to stuff the boots with clean straw, which would make the boots even warmer. She had rabbit-skin socks with the fur turned inside, and her parka had a good wolf-fur ruff to keep the wind from freezing her cheeks.

When she was very small, her mittens had been part of the parka, but now she wore nice little beaver mittens that were sewn to a long string that went around her neck so they couldn't be lost.

When there was no work for her to do, there was a new batch of sled-dog puppies to play with. Erinia would call, "Dzek, dzek, dzek," and they'd come running fast, tumbling over one another to get to her first.

Minook made her a little snow fort, and she and the puppies crawled in and out of it and pretended that it was their house.

Sometimes Erinia stood under the big spruce trees around the odinochka where the black ravens sat. She would imitate the calls they made, each one different from the last. Ravens knew a lot of different words, and Erinia wished she knew what they were saying.

Erinia liked to help the boys check the fish traps out under the ice in front of the odinochka. The fish froze immediately in strange shapes when they were dumped from the trap onto the ice, and Erinia would bring the circles and crescents of fish to Mamma in her little sled.

And when the moon was out and shining huge and bright on everything, she loved to slide down the riverbank on a piece of caribou hide, dried stiff and slick, the puppies racing alongside, snapping at her parka.

Sometimes when the sky was very black, she liked just to sit outdoors and look at the sharp, hard stars. On those nights it looked as if the stars had become much bigger and closer, and if she looked too long, they almost frightened her.

Every day, depending on the weather, the woods were different. Sometimes when the sun rose, every tree was coated with sparkling ice. Sometimes thick, soft snow fell for hours and coated every twig with a thin stack of snow. That was a good time to shake the trees so the load of snow would fall with a whispery *shlump*.

Erinia loved best the days when the frost on the trees turned to glittering crystals and with a shimmering sound gently drifted from the trees, throwing little sparks of colors in the bright sun.

But still, as much as she loved winter, she was always eager for spring.

Chapter Three

IN THE SPRING, AS SOON AS THE DAYS GREW LONGER, THE Russian American Company would always send three or four dog teams up the frozen river with the spring and summer's food and trade goods. It took four days for them to travel from Saint Michael, up to Unalakleet, and over the portage to the Yukon.

So when the days grew warmer, Erinia was restless, waiting and waiting for the company men to come.

"Oh, Papa, why don't they *hurry*?" she whined.

Papa laughed at her cross face. "Is there anyone more impatient than you, Erinia?"

Erinia made an even crosser face. "Maybe they'll never come," she said darkly.

But they always did come, and one bright morning from far away Erinia heard the little bells tinkling on the harnesses of the company dog teams.

All the dogs tied by the store began to yank on their tethers and bark their high-pitched visitor barks. The puppies sat back on their haunches with their ears twitching and their eyes wide. They weren't sure whether they should be afraid or excited.

And at last Erinia could see the teams coming up the river, and when it seemed she could stand waiting no longer, there they were, pulling up the steep bank in front of the store.

Lev was driving the first team. He pushed his frosted parka hood back and took off his wooden snow goggles and hollered at her in Russian: *"Maya malenkaya milashka!"* My little sweetheart!

Erinia beamed at him. She turned two cartwheels instead of saying anything, just to show how pleased she was.

Lev and Dimitri and Nikolai were the regular sled drivers. The other drivers would be different from trip to trip, sometimes Eskimo boys from the coast or Indian boys from Anvik, and they were nice too. But no one could be as much fun as Lev and Dimitri and Nikolai.

Stepan and Mikhail saw to the company dogs, unhitching them, giving them new spruce boughs to sleep on, seeing that they had water and dried fish.

Then while Lev and Dimitri and Nikolai drank tea with Mamma and Lena, Minook and Pitka and Elia and everyone else helped unload the sleds, because it was so exciting to see what was in the bundles the company had sent.

Erinia dashed back and forth between the sleds and the kitchen, where Mamma and Lena and the drivers were, beside herself with excitement. Mamma had to tell her over and over again not to get in anyone's way.

When all the packages were piled in the store, everyone went to help unwrap them.

As always there was tea. Bricks and bricks of tea.

Tea was the most important thing because everyone in Russian America had taken the Russian habit of drinking tea. Tea in the morning and all day long, and more tea at night.

There was flour, sugar, and salt, groats to make kasha, dried peas, lard, hardtack biscuits, and bouillon.

Erinia threw Papa a look of delight when she saw the box of canned peaches. The company didn't often send canned fruit because it was heavy and took up a lot of room, so it was wonderful when they did send it.

Besides the meat and fish and berries they got for themselves, these supplies would be all the food for the people in the odinochka until the fall and winter supplies were brought by boat from Saint Michael.

Next to tea the most important thing was tobacco. All the Indians used tobacco, and Old Man Kozevnikoff said the Indians and Eskimos had used it long before there were any Russian trading posts in Alaska. They'd gotten it from the Eskimos in Siberia.

Papa and Old Man Kozevnikoff smoked their pipes every chance they got, long-stemmed pipes with little brass bowls to hold the tobacco, which sent lazy little whiffs of sweet-smelling smoke twisting up toward the ceiling.

Papa said tobacco was good for your digestion, and Old Man Kozevnikoff said tobacco was good for your blood. But still they wouldn't let Erinia try it.

Papa and Old Man Kozevnikoff put the other things on the shelves around the store: soap, calico cloth, bullets and powder and caps for the muskets, flints, axes and Aleut hatchets, copper pitchers and big steel bowls, teapots, piles of white English wool blankets, muskets, shirts, dresses, and caps, and cast-iron pots.

Erinia loved the hats and caps, and tried them all on before Papa and Old Man Kozevnikoff could get them put away. She liked best the round, flat hats with fancy embroidery around the edges. They were called English smoking hats and they were very popular with the Indian men.

And of course there were the boxes of special trade

goods to admire—beads and buttons and jewelry. Erinia didn't know what to look at first.

While everyone else was unpacking, Mamma and Lena cooked, and when everything had been put away, they all ate a big supper at the table by the stove. Lev and Dimitri and Nikolai talked as fast as they could, interrupting one another and finishing one another's sentences, telling all the news.

They'd seen Kate for a minute at Ikogmute, and she was fine and said to tell her mamma and papa that she was studying hard.

Markovski, who ran the odinochka at Ikogmute, had died of a heart attack. Old Man Kozevnikoff, who had known him, looked sad and shook his head.

The company at Saint Michael had not received its quota of flour for bread from New Arkhangel, and so all the odinochkas would probably run short before next spring. Everyone around the table was sorry to hear that news because they were all used to eating bread at every meal. But of course it wasn't the first time they had not had enough flour. The last time it happened because the ship carrying the flour had come to grief.

Lukin, the explorer who worked for the Russian American Company like Papa and Old Man Kozevnikoff and the rest of them, was going all the way up the Yukon to the English odinochka at Fort Yukon. He was going to disguise himself as an Indian and look around to see what the English were doing up there. Perhaps they were selling liquor, which they were not supposed to do because they'd made an agreement with the Russians not to.

"What will happen if they are breaking their agreement?" Mamma asked. Everyone looked at her in surprise, for she hardly ever talked when people were around.

Lev lifted one shoulder a little. "It's up to the czar to decide what to do if they won't listen!"

A little line appeared between Mamma's eyes. *"Edzegee,"* she said. That meant she was afraid of what might happen.

Erinia was glad when they'd finally finished eating and talking, for then it was time for the music. Lev and Dimitri would play their instruments, and Nikolai would sing sad, throbbing songs from the Ukraine that he had learned from his Russian father.

Lev had a balalaika, a little triangle with strings, and Dimitri had a little accordion. When the song was a fast one, you couldn't see Lev's fingers, they moved so fast. Erinia sat pressed up next to him, trying to see how he played so fast, but she never could.

A small barrel of rum came with each shipment from Saint Michael. The men would drink it all and have headaches in the morning. When the rum was about halfway gone, Papa and Old Man Kozevnikoff and Stepan would feel they must dance the *kazachka*, the wild Russian Cossack dance they'd learned from their fathers. They couldn't do more than a few kicks before they fell on the floor gasping for air. Mamma and Lena sat on the benches and kept their fists jammed against their mouths, trying hard not to laugh at the men's dancing.

Erinia didn't mind laughing at them, though it wasn't polite.

Elia and Minook and Pitka tried it next. They were younger and could last longer, but none of them could dance as long as Lev and Dimitri. Mikhail had a lame foot, so he couldn't dance, but he clapped and roared encouragement at them.

Lev finally put the balalaika down and showed them how to do the kazachka properly, his arms folded across his chest, squatting down, his legs kicking out almost as fast as his fingers had flown, his boots thumping the floor to keep time with Dimitri's accordion.

And then he pulled Erinia off the bench and danced her around the room until she couldn't breathe anymore.

Lev still had dancing in his feet, though he'd worn nearly everyone out, but when he headed to the bench where Mamma and Lena were sitting, they shrieked and pressed themselves against the wall, refusing to dance. So Lev danced by himself until finally he'd had enough.

Then Nikolai sang his sad songs, which sounded like

someone crying. Some of his songs started out very slowly and got faster and faster, until Lev had to jump up and dance again. Some of his songs made Old Man Kozevnikoff cry.

"Ah, Mother Russia," he sighed, though Erinia knew he'd never been to Russia.

In the morning Dimitri and Lev and Nikolai loaded up the sleds with all the furs Papa and Old Man Kozevnikoff had gotten in trade during the winter. They would take them back to the company store at Saint Michael. From there the furs would be taken by ship down to New Arkhangel, where the headquarters of the company was, and they'd be sold all over the world.

"Imagine," said Dimitri. "Some little girl somewhere in the world will wear these furs you played with."

Erinia tried to imagine American and Russian and English children wearing coats and hats made with those furs, but she just couldn't.

She'd never seen a Russian or English or American child, so she didn't know what they'd look like.

Chapter Four

AFTER THE COMPANY MEN LEFT, THE NIGHTS GREW SHORTER and shorter, until there was almost no night left.

At bedtime Erinia had a hard time going to sleep because the sun was still shining in the mica windows. It seemed to Erinia after the long darkness of winter that she was wasting daylight if she wasn't outside.

After Mamma sent her to bed, Erinia sang all the songs she knew, very loudly. Then she kicked the heavy caribou covering off the bed and threw her rabbit-skin blanket on the floor. Then she drummed her heels on the wall until Mamma came to quiet her.

"*Kaa*," said Mamma. Stop that. "Every spring you go half wild, Erinia."

Sometimes Papa would come and tell her stories, to help her get to sleep. She always asked for the same stories, told in the same way.

"Tell me about New Arkhangel, Papa," she said. That was the town where Papa grew up, far away in the south of Russian America.

New Arkhangel had always seemed to Erinia a perfect name for a town with such fancy houses with carpets, where ladies dressed in red gowns.

The Russian church, Papa said, was full of gold-trimmed books and gold-embroidered cloth hangings and icons studded with jewels. In the church hundreds of candles made a wonderful, soft light and the priest burned a special powder to make smoke that smelled good.

Papa showed her with his hands how the church tower was shaped, round and pointed on the top and swollen fat at the bottom. A round tower seemed wonderful to Erinia.

Papa's mother had been a Tlingit Indian and his father had been a Russian.

"My father had a big black beard," said Papa, "but his mustache was red, like a fox, and his eyebrows were yellow!"

Erinia liked having a grandfather like that, all different colors.

"Tell me what he called you, Papa," said Erinia.

"He called me Vanyusha," said Papa. Erinia always

smiled to think of her big papa being so little he could be called a baby name for Ivan.

Papa told her about the tall totem poles his mother's people carved, and about the costumes they wore for celebrations, beautiful red cloaks with yellow ravens and bears woven into them.

Papa's mother had died when he was very young.

"Tell me what she looked like, Papa."

"I can't remember anything about her," Papa said, as he always did. Erinia was never happy with that answer. She was sure if he tried hard, he'd remember something.

"Well, didn't your father tell you *one* thing about her?"

"No, nothing," said Papa.

Erinia felt very sad for Papa's mother, not to be remembered. It frightened her to think of being forgotten like that.

The Russian American Company educated all the part-Russian children born in Russian America so they would learn a trade. Because he was the child of a Russian, Papa had been taken to live in the children's barracks very early so he could start his education. Papa was good at figuring and wrote perfect slanting letters, so he became a clerk.

When Papa was doing his book work, Erinia sat near him so she could watch his pen dip and glide over the paper.

When he taught her to write the Russian letters, her pen had stuttered and splatted ink all over the paper, and the ink had run down like tears from the bottoms of the letters. She got better at it as she grew older, but she was sure she would never be able to write as beautifully as Papa did.

When the Russians first came to Alaska, a hundred years before, the Russian hunters killed so many seals and sea otters in the ocean that soon there were no more to be killed. So then the company began to build forts and odinochkas along the rivers in the north, where there were still furs. That was why they sent Papa when he was a young man way up north on the Yukon to help run the store at Nulato with Old Man Kozevnikoff.

"Tell me how hard it was when you came here, Papa."

"In New Arkhangel," he said, "we were waited on. Our meals were cooked for us and set on the table. The dishes were washed by the kitchen people, our clothes were washed and mended for us. I had never been hungry. I found what hard work it was just to keep alive up here. I was a clerk! I'd never even been hunting!"

"And the first time you saw a moose, you thought it was a horse!"

"That's right."

"Maybe the first time I see a horse, I'll think it's a moose," Erinia said. Papa smiled.

"And you were very cold!" she reminded him.

"Very," said Papa. "I never dreamed of such cold. But Lena made sure I had good, warm clothes, the kind we didn't need in New Arkhangel."

"And then you met Mamma."

"And then I met Mamma."

"Tell me about Mamma," said Erinia.

Papa folded his arms across his chest and looked at the ceiling. "Mamma was quiet and serious, and she knew how to do everything," said Papa. "She was always busy, always working."

Then Papa looked at Erinia with a smug little smile.

"And of course she thought I was very handsome."

Erinia laughed so hard at this that she had to stop and cough, while Papa pretended that he was insulted that she'd laughed.

Papa had taken Mamma downriver to Ikogmute the first chance he got, so Mamma could be baptized by Father Netsvetov and he could marry them. The priest had given her a Russian name, Marina, but Papa always called her *Malanka*, little one.

They started having children right away. Because Erinia was the youngest, she couldn't remember the ones who had died.

"It was very hard to keep babies alive in those days," Papa said sadly. Three had died and only three were left when Erinia was born: Pitka and Minook and Kate.

35

"Tell about the medicine man, Papa."

"The medicine man told us to give you away because we had bad luck raising children. 'Give her to someone else who has better luck,' he said, 'or maybe even the ones who are living will die as well.'"

But Papa didn't believe in medicine men and didn't like them one bit.

"Give my Erinia away?" said Papa with a fierce look.

Erinia smiled, as she always did at this part. "But wasn't the medicine man mad, Papa, when you didn't do what he said?"

Papa said he gave the medicine man a nice present and let him go away feeling pleased with himself, which was good for trade.

Erinia's eyes were heavy now, and she closed them. No matter how many times Papa told her his stories, she would never get tired of them.

They were her stories too.

As soon as she got outside in the morning, Erinia pushed her hood off and let her mittens dangle by their strings. Soon her ears were red and her little hands were rough and chapped, and Mamma scolded her when she saw them, but Erinia didn't listen.

She wanted to wear as few clothes as possible in the warm spring sun.

With her hood off she could hear everything. In the spring sounds got louder and louder as the snow melted: Mikhail's ax in the birch grove, a raven squawking across the river, Old Man Kozevnikoff calling across the yard to Lena. Every sound was crisp and new in the spring.

The sun melted the snow a little during the day, and when the sun went down at night, the melted snow would freeze again, making a hard crust for easy traveling. You didn't even need snowshoes then.

Every afternoon Erinia and Mamma walked across that hard crust on top of the deep snow to gather pitch from the spruce trees.

Mamma knocked the pitch off the trees with a stick, and Erinia collected the pieces of pitch from the bottom of the trees and put them in her basket.

It was nesting season for the squirrels, and they were chasing one another so furiously that they hardly paid attention to Erinia and Mamma. They looked so funny spiraling around and around the trees, ratcheting all the way in their language, which sounded like swearing. Or dashing across the snow, one so close to the other that they looked like an orange streak.

Erinia couldn't stop watching them.

"Erinia, pay attention or you won't see where the pitch has fallen!" Mamma scolded.

Spruce pitch was good for everything. You used it to seal the seams of canoes and baskets and to heal wounds. The clear kind was the best for cuts. You had to chop open the tree to get that. The yellow kind, which ran down the outside of the tree, was good to chew and tasted like spruce wood smelled, sharp and bitter.

The Eskimos would trade almost anything for spruce pitch because in their country there were no trees. If Erinia and Mamma gathered a lot of pitch, they could trade it for good waterproof sealskin boot soles, thick walrus leather, seal hides, seal oil, and whale meat, or even for an Eskimo parka made of *cikigpak*. Everyone wanted a parka like that, made from the skins of the little ground squirrels that the Eskimos had in their country.

So Mamma and Erinia worked hard all week until they had so much that they felt rich.

Chapter Five

FAR AWAY ACROSS THE WIDE RIVER, NEAR THE BLUE KAIYUH Mountains, were the scattered winter camps of the Indian families. In the spring they'd come to the odinochka with the furs they'd trapped during the winter, and then they'd rest for a bit before they went to their spring camps.

Everyone at the odinochka was happy to see the Kaiyuh people come after the long winter months. Mamma was happy because she could visit with her relatives, and Elia and Minook and Pitka were happy because they liked to talk to the girls.

Erinia was happy because Nilaat would come. When Erinia and Nilaat were just babies, they had been set together to play in the dirt in front of the odinochka, and since then they had been friends.

Nilaat had long black braids, and when she smiled, her eyes squinted up into little crescents of blackness in her brown, brown face.

No one spoiled Nilaat. She was an orphan, and orphans were often not treated as well as other children. Erinia knew that if she lived Nilaat's life, she would be in a temper all the time.

Mamma had asked to have Nilaat when she was orphaned, but an old woman who was a relative of Nilaat's mother wanted her.

"Who will work for me if you take her?" Kkaabaa had asked Mamma in a mean way.

Mamma felt sorry for Nilaat and looked out for her as best she could. Last year she'd made a doll for her, just like Erinia's, dressed in a tiny little parka and boot-pants.

This past winter she'd made Nilaat summer moccasins with blue beads on the toes. Erinia knew just how Nilaat would smile when she saw those moccasins.

Finally one morning, before anyone was even out of bed, from far off downriver they heard shooting. That was the Indian way of saying they were coming.

Elia and Minook and Pitka ran to the store to get their guns. They rushed down to the riverbank, leaping over logs and canoes with their long legs, scrambling down the bank to shoot their guns off too.

That was how they said hurry, and you're most welcome.

The Indians had been traveling all night, when the trail was hard, which was a smart thing to do in the spring, when the snow was so soft during the day.

A long line of people and sleds was coming on the trail. The sleds were piled with beaver pelts, and the babies and very young children rode on top of the loads.

Women and children pulled most of the sleds, but a few sleds were pulled by a single big dog. Pack dogs, fitted with bundles that were tied around their middles, trotted along beside some of the sleds.

Nilaat must be one of the children with packs at the end of the long line, though Erinia couldn't tell them apart from so far away.

"Nilaat!" Erinia yelled, even though she knew Nilaat couldn't hear her.

The Kaiyuh men walked along by the sleds, empty-handed except for their spears and guns.

Papa said that in the old days, when he first came to Nulato, all the Indian men had carried spears because they had no guns. The spears were made of Palma knives, from Yakuts in Siberia, attached with thongs to long wooden shafts.

Erinia thought they were very pretty, the tops of the knives designed like the curls of rams' horns. But she could never touch one, because Mamma said if a woman or girl touched the men's weapons, this would bring bad luck.

The men were never without their spears in those days, even if they went just a short distance. They never let their guard down, Papa said, for fear of attack by enemies.

Only the old men carried spears now.

Everyone, men and women and children, still used bows and arrows to hunt small game. You wouldn't want to waste a shell on something small, like a rabbit or a bird.

But now the younger men all carried guns, muskets that had to be loaded with powder.

Erinia didn't like guns or the noise they made or the sharp smell they left in the air.

When their sleds were pulled up in front of the open gate, the Kaiyuh men unloaded their beaver skins and took them into the store. Then they took the sleds a half mile downriver to settle into the three big underground houses where they always stayed when they were in Nulato.

Nilaat finally came up the bank, carrying a load wrapped in a caribou skin on her back. The wide strap that supported the load pressed against her forehead. Erinia ran to her and helped her lift the bundle to set it down, and then she reached out to touch Nilaat's cheek.

"Nilaat," she said. *"Gganaa."* My friend.

Nilaat gave Erinia a delighted smile. She'd been walking with that heavy load, little skinny Nilaat, and she still had that smile.

"I'm here at last," said Nilaat.

Between them Nilaat and Erinia carried the bundle all the way to the winter houses, chattering so fast they were nearly breathless when they got there.

Nilaat stopped short in the trail to open her mouth wide. "Look!" She pointed to a new hole where a tooth had been.

Then Erinia showed Nilaat the place on the bottom of her mouth where two teeth were missing. She pushed her tongue against it to show that her tongue could stick out of the hole.

Mamma and Lena and the boys walked with the Kaiyuh people too, asking questions, about the trapping this year, about the conditions of the trail, about someone who'd been sick.

Erinia felt almost dizzy with so many people around her all at once, with so much talking to listen to. Everyone was busy, moving here and there to do what needed to be done.

After the dogs were unhitched, each was tethered to a tree by a tie-rod. The bundles were unloaded, the empty sleds were heaved up onto the sled racks, and the children were peeled out of their heavy trail clothes.

Erinia helped Nilaat take her bundle down into one of the houses. These were underground houses with just the top showing, like a smooth, round hill. To go in, you had to bend over and creep down a little low passageway to get to the ladder, then climb down the ladder to a big open room. Papa and Old Man Kozevnikoff had been raised like Russians in log houses, and they didn't like these underground houses. They thought they were dirty and dark and miserable. And smoky. But Mamma looked a dark look at them when they said that and told them that underground houses were much warmer than the log house they lived in now.

It *was* smoky inside if someone was cooking. Then you had to turn your face to the ground, where you could breathe good air. But Erinia didn't mind that. She liked to visit in the underground houses and see all the old-fashioned things the Kaiyuh people used. They still used caribou bladders to carry water and oil, and they made beautifully decorated quivers for arrows from caribou hide. Some of the old people even had fire drills instead of flints or iron to strike sparks.

Everything was in its special bag. This seemed to Erinia to be a very good arrangement, and when she visited in the houses, she would ask to see what was in this bag or that, until the grown-ups got impatient with her and shooed her outside.

The women had fish-skin bags filled with net-making tools and little caribou-skin bags heavy with cooking stones. They had to heat the stones in the fire and then drop them into a birch-bark basket filled with meat and water. They would do that over and over again until the water boiled and the meat was cooked. It took a long time.

Old Seyula had a blackfish-skin bag that held a drawknife made of two beaver teeth. He used the knife to scrape spruce roots and to make smooth wooden bowls. Erinia loved to see him use that knife.

And Kkaabaa, when she wasn't cross, would show Erinia the stone lamp that had belonged to her mother and her grandmother before her. "Everywhere she went," Kkaabaa said, "to winter camp, to muskrat camp, to the hunting grounds, everywhere she went my mother carried this lamp."

It must have taken months and months to hollow out the place in the stone where the lump of fat or fish oil was put. People in the old days must have had more patience. Now everyone used square scraps of tin bent up at the edges to hold fat for burning. It was fast to make a lamp like that, but it wasn't the same.

Nilaat would look curiously at Erinia when she asked to see the lamp. She couldn't see anything interesting in it.

"It's so old," Erinia said, trying to explain. Nothing in Erinia's life was old. Things made of wood, and birch bark or skin, didn't last long enough to get old. This stone lamp was the only old thing she'd ever seen.

After everyone had put their things away in the winter houses, Erinia knew there would be a dance of hello.

The Indians had a dance or a song for everything. They weren't supposed to start anything without doing the proper dance or song.

There were dances of hello and dances of good-bye. There were songs to make the snow melt faster or to make it come, dances for making the lightning and thunder stop, songs for hunting, and dances for fishing.

But some of the young men were so eager to start trading their furs that they started off for the odinochka without waiting for the dance. When Simaaga saw them walking up the trail, he thundered after them and gave them a terrible tongue-lashing for forgetting about the dance.

He was short and thick and stood absolutely straight. His black eyes were fierce. He was the medicine man, and many people were afraid of him. Erinia certainly was.

He said that the young were forgetting the ways of their fathers, that they had no manners anymore, that they would be the cause of terrible things for everyone because they were ruining the luck with their disrespectful behavior.

Erinia hid behind Mamma as best she could while Simaaga shouted, his face dark with anger. She thought if she had been the one he'd yelled at, she might have fainted. But when the young men followed him back to stand in the line for the dancing, she saw that they sent merry looks at one another behind the old man's back.

All the grown-ups made a line facing the east, and the ones who were wearing feathers pulled them out of their hair and held them in both hands. Then they began to sing the song, leaning forward as they stamped their right feet, their long braids whipping.

The stamping was so steady and hard that Erinia could feel the vibrations right up through her moccasins.

Simaaga was in the center of the line. He had put eagle down in his white hair to dress up, and he began to jerk back and forth, barking and yelping and howling like a wolf, squawking like a raven. Erinia didn't like this part of the dance. She looked at Nilaat, but Simaaga didn't seem to worry Nilaat at all.

When the dance was over, it was time to trade, and most of the people began to walk to the odinochka. Erinia pulled Nilaat by the sleeve. "Nilaat, Mamma made you beautiful new moccasins. Come and try them on."

But Kkaabaa frowned at Erinia and waved her away. "Go with them," she said. "Nilaat has work to do. She can't be bothered with you."

Nilaat always hauled the water and gathered the firewood. She had the hardest work to do because she was an orphan. But Nilaat never seemed to mind. She did her work cheerfully.

"I'll come when I've finished my work," she said.

So Erinia said good-bye and left Nilaat there to work.

Chapter Six

A T THE ODINOCHKA THE KAIYUH PEOPLE CROWDED INTO the store, excited, touching this and that, looking to see what new things there were. Erinia squeezed in among them, but she was afraid she'd be stepped on. She climbed up on the wooden flour barrels and from there to the top of the big counter, where she sat with her legs tucked under her. She was glad Mamma wasn't in the store to see her sitting on the counter.

Old Man Kozevnikoff, taller than anyone in the room, his big belly straining the front of his high-necked Russian shirt, lumbered around the store, greeting everyone with the greatest joy, loud and jolly and making a joke of everything.

He seized Simaaga by the shoulders and kissed him soundly on both cheeks in the Russian way.

Simaaga almost looked as if he was going to smile. It was impossible to be cross with Old Man Kozevnikoff.

Old Man Kozevnikoff teased the women and held up earrings by their faces and told them they would look beautiful with these earrings or that.

He made the babies scream with fear, he was so loud. But the older children watched him with wide-eyed smiles. They remembered him from last time, and they knew he would have some special treat for them before the day was over.

Papa liked things quiet, but Old Man Kozevnikoff was so glad to see the families from across the river that Erinia wondered if he would have been happier if he had lived in a bigger place, where there were a lot of people.

A young woman with a baby on her back came to Erinia where she was sitting on the counter. Her name was Deetza and she was always very crabby with Nilaat and Erinia. Deetza took off her baby strap and pulled the baby out of her parka hood. She handed him to Erinia. "Here, keep him for me," she ordered. Erinia frowned. She didn't like Deetza's bossy ways and she didn't want to hold her sour-smelling baby. But she put him on her lap and let him watch the commotion with her.

When it was time to get down to business, Papa and

Old Man Kozevnikoff started to trade. They measured each beaver pelt, turned it over, snapped the pelt to see if it crackled, checked the guard hairs, and looked serious.

Certain items cost a certain number of beaver skins. A musket cost the most. Old Man Kozevnikoff would hold a musket upright, and the skins had to stack up as high as the top of the musket barrel.

People had other things to trade as well as beaver skins, like *babiche*. Babiche was leather strips cut in a spiral out of a caribou or moose hide. It was used to bind the parts of a sled together, to weave the latticework on snowshoes, and to attach the stone heads of tools to wooden handles. Babiche was used for everything, so Papa and Old Man Kozevnikoff were glad to get it.

There were wolverine and wolf pelts, which were very good for ruffs, and a few marten and mink, lynx and otter and fox.

Two of the old men had some tool handles to trade. These were made of wood that had been hardened slowly in the fire until it was almost rock hard. It took a long time to make these handles, so they were very valuable.

They traded for tea and tobacco, calico dresses and shirts, steel bowls, blankets. These were all things that were light and could be carried easily. The Indians traveled all year round, carrying everything they owned, so what they owned could not be heavy or unnecessary.

An iron pot made cooking easier, but it was heavy, and for that reason not everyone wanted one. But Erinia thought it must be very hard to cook in the old way, with cooking stones in birch-bark baskets.

Deetza brought her baby a bell that she'd gotten in trade. He couldn't make it ring because he held it wrong, so Erinia shook it for him to make him laugh. A little more noise in the store wouldn't make any difference.

Everyone loved to trade with Old Man Kozevnikoff. He was never stingy, and when he wrapped up packages of tea, he'd throw in a little extra. "Some for the pot," he always said.

But if they asked for too many things for their furs, Old Man Kozevnikoff would strike his forehead with his hand and bellow, "Nyet, nyet, nyet," and they would have to come down a little, until they reached the right amount.

It was very funny to watch, like a game, because everyone knew Old Man Kozevnikoff was just pretending to be angry.

He expected people to ask for too much.

In the next few days after the trading was finished, Erinia's house and the store were full of people, talking and laughing and eating.

They all liked to have Mamma make tea in the samovar, and they liked to drink it with lots of sugar.

The women sat in the kitchen with Mamma and sewed and gossiped and smoked their pipes while they watched her work.

Mamma not only had her Indian jobs to do, she had her Russian jobs too. The women from the Kaiyuh thought she was very overworked when they saw her scrubbing at the washboard, turning out loaves and loaves of bread, scouring the planks of the kitchen floor with sand, shining the mica windows, washing the tin cups and plates and cutlery. "*Kuklaa,*" they said. Poor thing.

They wouldn't like to be Mamma, that was for sure.

But Mamma said sharply that she wouldn't like to be like them and have to pull the sleds and carry the wood, either.

If someone criticized the Russian ways, Mamma fretted. And if someone criticized the Indian ways, Mamma fretted. Erinia thought it must be very confusing to be Mamma.

Mamma said she was Erinia's age when she and her people had come to fish at Nulato as they always did, but one time there was something new on the riverbank. Mamma said they all stood and stared at it for a long time. It was the first log house they'd ever seen. The men of Mamma's band burned that log house down, but the next time they came, the Russians had built another, and this time traders were living there. And from that time on, things began to change.

Mamma worried about change. "When I was a girl, there was a right way and a wrong way," she often said. "Now everything is all mixed up."

Chapter Seven

NILAAT FINALLY FINISHED HER WORK AND KKAABAA LET her come to see Erinia. Mamma gave Nilaat the summer moccasins she'd made for her. Nilaat stroked the blue beads sewn on the toe and then smiled her biggest smile at Mamma. "You are very good to me." Mamma smiled and put her hand on Nilaat's head. Then she turned back to her work.

"I can't wait for summer to wear them," Nilaat said to Erinia.

Kkaabaa could sometimes be persuaded to let Nilaat stay with Erinia at night. It wouldn't do if Nilaat asked, or Erinia, so they always got Old Man Kozevnikoff to ask her.

"Grandmother," he'd cry. "We miss our little Nilaat when she's gone. Will you let us have her company for this one night, to eat with us and keep us cheerful?"

Kkaabaa would always grumble, "I will need her. Who's to get the water?" And Old Man Kozevnikoff would say soothingly, "You'll never miss her. She'll come back to you early in the morning!" And then he would say, "And of course, she will bring you tobacco for your pipe."

So Kkaabaa would say Nilaat could stay the night, and when the old woman couldn't see them, Erinia and Nilaat would hug each other and dance a little joyous dance on their tiptoes.

Nilaat was very glad to eat Russian food, and Mamma would always put out something special for her, maybe canned peaches or a bowl of kasha.

And Old Man Kozevnikoff would make *blinis* for them when Nilaat was there, little Russian pancakes served with sugared blueberries that had been stored since the fall in birch-bark baskets.

Nilaat would help Erinia with her chores after dinner, and then they would sit by the big stove in the store talking and playing with their dolls. Nilaat's was still perfect, its little wooden face smooth and clean, and the tiny clothes nicely cared for. Erinia's doll was not so perfect and had lost most of the features painted on her face because

Erinia had left her in a puddle one day. And her doll's boot-pants were lost as well. Mamma pinched her lips together when she saw Erinia's doll.

When they were ready to sleep, Erinia gave Nilaat a cotton nightgown to sleep in. She made a face at Nilaat's rabbit underwear. She was glad she didn't have to wear that next to her skin. She was glad she had her good Russian underwear.

"But it's very warm," said Nilaat.

"But the rabbit skin sheds, and the hair sticks to you," said Erinia.

Nilaat shrugged. "It's warm," she said cheerfully.

They slept in Erinia's little log bed under the caribou coverlet and talked nearly all night long.

Nilaat said that one of the girls in her band was in seclusion because she had begun menstruating, and Nilaat told Erinia all about it. That girl had to be in isolation for a year, and no one could come near her except one old woman. She couldn't drink anything but water, and she must sip it through a swan's-bone straw that hung around her neck at all times.

She had to wear a special hood for that year so that she couldn't look at anyone and they couldn't look at her. She wore porcupine feet next to her skin so that she could have her babies easily, and the only fresh meat she could eat for the whole year was porcupine meat.

When they traveled, she couldn't look at the river and she couldn't walk on the same trails as everyone else.

She could never come near any men or their tools or their canoes because she could take away all their luck in hunting and fishing. She could make them weak, like women.

She could never take off or change her clothes during this year.

Erinia looked at Nilaat in horror. "A whole *year*?" She couldn't think of anything worse than wearing the same dirty clothes for a year.

"Papa won't make me do that," Erinia said, but she was really half afraid that he might go along with Mamma if Mamma insisted on the old ways.

"When I become a woman, I will leave Kkaabaa and I'll come here," said Nilaat. "Then I won't have to do it either."

Erinia frowned. "How long will it be before it happens to us?" she asked. Nilaat thought for a minute. "Maybe four more summers."

"Oh," said Erinia, very relieved that it would be so long.

Erinia and Nilaat loved to talk about the things they'd do when they were grown up, when Nilaat would come to live in Nulato.

Nilaat said they both would get married to some hard-working boys, good hunters, and have babies that would play together in the dirt outside the odinochka, just the way she and Erinia had done.

Erinia thought about all the hard work Mamma did, and so she said that they wouldn't get married *right* away.

"First we'll go to New Arkhangel to see the beautiful houses."

"Edzegee," said Nilaat. I'd be too scared.

"We'll see the carpets and the ladies with red dresses," Erinia said.

Nilaat raised her eyebrows. "What's a *carpet*?"

Erinia had asked Papa the same question.

"It's a thick, thick cloth, thicker than a moose hide, made of woven wool, in all sorts of beautiful colors and patterns. They put this carpet on the floor, so they don't walk on just bare boards. When you walk on it, your steps don't make a noise, and you don't even need to wear your shoes, it's so soft and warm."

Nilaat's face was serious while she tried to imagine a carpet. Then she smiled.

"I'd like to see a carpet so much," she said.

Chapter Eight

Soon the Indians had to leave to go back to the Kaiyuh country for caribou. After the caribou hunt they'd cross the Innoko River while it was still frozen and build skin boats from the caribou hides. When the ice in the grass lakes melted away, they would hunt beaver and muskrat. Then the geese and ducks would come back north and the hungry part of the year would be over.

Erinia stood with Papa on the riverbank and watched them go. There was a heavy place in her chest, watching Nilaat go across the river with the others, that big pack on her back. She wished Nilaat were spoiled the way she was. And the odinochka seemed so empty without her.

Papa pulled her braids gently. "Cheer up. Soon Nilaat

and the others will be back for the whole summer, to fish."

"I know, but it doesn't *seem* like soon, Papa."

But she knew, really, that spring was such a busy time, there would have been no time for her and Nilaat to be together.

There were a hundred things to do.

The trees were bare of snow, and all the icicles from the store building had fallen into the soft, tired snow beneath them. Water dripped from the eaves now, and the snow had become grainy and didn't glitter in the morning sun.

That snow melted fast, shrinking away from the sides of the store building, and when it was nearly gone, Stepan and Papa went off into the hills to hunt for caribou. Almost all of their dry meat was gone, and what dried fish was left had to be saved for the dogs.

No matter how scarce food was, there was always plenty of blackfish, which Mikhail trapped in the grass lakes. Sometimes they ate those, but most of the time they fed them to the dogs. Blackfish didn't taste like much.

The only meat they had was from the rabbits and ptarmigan Mamma had snared. It was the women's job to bring home small animals and the men's job to hunt for the big ones.

When Erinia caught her first rabbit in a snare she set by herself, she was very proud.

Mamma was proud too and made a little ceremony for her, which was the custom with her people. She roasted the rabbit on a stick and everyone at the odinochka had a piece, and they all said it was the most delicious rabbit they'd ever tasted.

Then Mamma and Erinia tanned the little brown skin, and with that skin and one other they made rabbit-skin socks for Erinia to wear inside her boots in the winter.

But sometimes in the spring rabbits were very scarce, and the ptarmigan and grouse, too. Those were hungry times when that happened, because the salmon hadn't come yet. But they were never as hungry as people who lived off the land, because they had the store.

"Once when I was a little girl we had nothing to eat in the spring but the white insides of willows, and the babiche from our sleds and snowshoes," Mamma told her. Erinia could not imagine how you could eat babiche, no matter how hungry you were, but Mamma said that after you'd eaten the babiche, you would have to eat your boot soles next. So Erinia knew that there was something worse than eating babiche.

Neither Erinia nor Mamma snared anything for a while after that rabbit, and everyone was tired of bread and blackfish, though of course they didn't complain. Then Mikhail caught a lynx and everyone smiled to think there would be meat for dinner that night.

Mamma skinned the lynx and cut it into pieces to boil in the big pot outdoors. It smelled so good as it was cooking that Erinia stood over the pot and breathed in the steam.

But Mamma frowned at her and told her to get away from the pot. She said women and girls must never eat lynx meat. It was *hutlaanee*, forbidden, and so Erinia had to watch the men eat that delicious meat and not have a bit herself. It made her very cross.

Everyone in the odinochka tried not to break Mamma's rules, because breaking them worried her so.

In the Athabascan way everything had a spirit, even the rocks and trees and river. These spirits must not be offended or bad things would happen.

The bones of each animal must be treated with respect or the hunter wouldn't catch that animal again for a long time. It would turn its back on you, was what Mamma said.

There were special words to be said when you slipped the beaver's bones back into the water, special words to be said to the birch when you took its bark.

You must stay awake while people were skinning beaver nearby. To fall asleep would be disrespectful. You must not whistle at night, you must never brag. Fish could not be fed to dogs on the day they were caught. A flying squirrel would bring terrible luck. Women and girls could never eat certain parts of the bear or beaver or wolverine. Or any part of a lynx.

How could you remember all those things? There was no end to the rules, and Erinia wished there weren't any at all.

Chapter Nine

AFTER STEPAN AND PAPA LEFT TO GO HUNTING, THE Aodinochka yard turned to thick, horrible mud, which Erinia knew would suck her moccasins off if she went near it. That had happened to her when she was very little. Mikhail and the boys put down split logs for everyone to walk on.

The ice on the river was rotten and there were standing pools of water all over it. And then one day the ice began to break up, and then it began to move downriver, the cakes of ice grinding against one another, making a fearful noise. Some years the ice went out smoothly, calm and well behaved. But this year the ice was rowdy and noisy and gave a lot of trouble.

While Erinia stood in front of the store watching the moving ice, she saw that one of the slabs of ice had been thrown upside down and the underneath ice had formed deep blue jewel-like crystals. It was so beautiful in the evening light that she had to run down to the sandbar to look at it closer.

Elia was in the wood yard splitting wood when he saw Erinia go down the bank. He shouted at her, but the sound of the ice was so loud that she couldn't hear. He threw down his ax and started down the bank after her.

As Erinia stood on the sandbar a huge piece of ice, as big as the bathhouse, stopped short in the river, blocked by more ice. Behind that piece a slab of ice as big as the first crashed into it and slid onto the top of it.

Before Erinia knew what was happening, the top piece of ice was tumbling onto the sandbar. It teetered on its edge for a moment before it fell over.

Erinia was so shocked that the ice slab suddenly looked so big standing on edge like that, she forgot to move and run away. Elia reached the sandbar at that moment, and he jerked her up by the parka just as the ice fell on the spot where she'd been standing.

She knew, as Elia carried her over his shoulder up to the store, bumping and slamming against his back, that she'd been very bad. What if the ice had fallen on her? What if it had fallen on Elia, who was only trying to help her?

Lena began to weep when Elia told her what had happened, and she hugged Erinia fiercely. "Oh, Erinia, what would your papa say to you? You could have been crushed!"

Mamma stood stiff and scowling. "What were you thinking of, you foolish child?" she asked in a dreadful voice.

Even Old Man Kozevnikoff looked grieved by her carelessness. And her disobedience.

Erinia listened to them with her head down and tears streaking down her face.

She wished she could start the morning all over so that all day long she would be careful and remember what she'd been told, so no one could find fault with her. It was so embarrassing to be told that you were foolish. Erinia didn't want to be foolish. She wanted to be smarter and wiser than anyone.

The ice fought and pushed and crashed its way downriver all that night and for one whole day before it began to jam up. There was an island in the river across from the odinochka, and the ice slabs piled up against that island, making a big wall of ice that dammed the water.

Old Man Kozevnikoff and Mikhail and the boys stood on the bank, watching the river anxiously. Then the dammed river rose suddenly, covering the sandbars and climbing fast up the bank in front of the odinochka.

They all ran in different directions. Old Man Kozevnikoff yelled at Lena to get ready. Mamma shrieked, and she and Lena ran to pile all the pots and pans and dishes on the top shelves in the kitchen. Then Mamma ran up the watchtower stairs to store the things that wouldn't fit on the shelves. Lena was much too fat to run up and down those stairs, so she carried things out into the yard and left them by the steps of the watchtower so they'd be there when Mamma was ready for another load.

Minook yelled, "Erinia, come grab these dogs!" and she hurried to help him. Minook put his fingers under the collars of the two biggest dogs and ran with them up to the top of the hill behind the odinochka, where they'd be out of harm's way if it flooded. Erinia put a rope on the mother dog's collar and scrambled with her up the hill. The puppies followed behind their mother, not at all bothered by the fuss. While Minook tethered the dogs, Erinia ran back and got the last dog, who was by this time looking very worried that he'd be left behind.

Pitka and Mikhail grabbed up the things in the odinochka yard, the saws and axes and sawhorses, and carried them up the stairs to the other watchtower. They left the heavy little blacksmith forge for Elia to bring, and he carried it up those steep stairs, grunting and red faced.

Old Man Kozevnikoff came out of the store, where he'd been piling trade goods on the top shelves. "When

68

you've finished with the yard, come and get the furs out of the storeroom," he shouted at them.

"Shall we put them in the watchtower?" asked Pitka.

Old Man Kozevnikoff thought for a moment. "No. High ground, I think. Those watchtower roofs might leak. We can't have the furs wet."

Minook and Erinia ran with the men to the storeroom. Old Man Kozevnikoff changed his mind when they got there. "Mikhail and Elia, you help the women get the food ready to take up the hill. We'll need enough for at least a week. Minook, you and Erinia take care of the furs. Erinia's big enough to help you while I clear out the store." Erinia stood up straighter to make herself look even bigger.

Minook stuffed a canvas bag with marten skins for Erinia to carry.

"Don't drag it on the ground or let it get wet," he said. "It's heavy, but hold it high. And then come back for some more." It *was* heavy, but Erinia didn't care. Nothing in the odinochka was so valuable as those furs. Minook piled furs into Mamma's canoe while Erinia took the first load up, and then he dragged it to the hill while Erinia trotted after him with another bag of furs slung over her shoulder. It was so heavy that if she stopped, it pulled her off balance, so she tried not to stop. Minook spread out the fish-skin tarp to keep the furs off the ground.

She was thinking about Papa and Stepan out hunting.

They were so late. They should have been back a week ago. Maybe something had happened to them. Maybe they'd be drowned when the water rose. Maybe they were already drowned. She ran to catch up with Minook.

"Oh, Minook, what will happen to Papa and Stepan? Will they be safe?" Her voice was jagged from running and her words came out in gasps.

"Of course," grumbled Minook. He didn't look at her. "They have sense enough to get to high ground."

But Erinia knew that sometimes the floodwaters came so quickly there was no time to run. And she could tell from Minook's voice that he was worried too.

When all of them had put everything valuable out of harm's way, they stood on the riverbank and watched the water rise slowly, inch by inch, hoping and hoping that the ice dam would break.

When it looked as if it would surely flood, Old Man Kozevnikoff and Elia set up two caribou-skin tents on the hill where the dogs were tied. They would need a dry place to sleep when the water came up into the odinochka and covered their beds.

The water rose, slowly and steadily, until in places the bank began to crumble into the angry water.

When Old Man Kozevnikoff saw that, he said, "Go up to the tents." And just as they turned to go up the hill and leave the odinochka to the cold, muddy water, the dam of ice broke apart with a noise like a rifle shot.

No one said anything for a minute, they were so relieved. Then Mikhail said in a disgusted way, "All that work for nothing." And they all laughed as hard as they could, because it was true.

The water dropped immediately and the milky brown river slid on, leaving chunks of ice stranded on the sandbars and islands.

Within hours the whole desolate riverbank was strewn with driftwood, huge logs and twisted branches, all coated with slimy mud. Erinia thought it looked very ugly.

And then they began the job of bringing everything back to the odinochka.

"It's much easier to bring things down a hill than it is to take them up a hill," said Old Man Kozevnikoff. And that should have been true, but it wasn't. When they were running to beat the floodwaters, they hardly knew how tired they were, they hardly felt anything. Now they weren't afraid, but they were tired and hadn't had enough to eat for a long time, and so the work seemed very hard. They all moved very slowly.

Erinia helped Minook load the furs back into Mamma's canoe, and together they dragged the canoe down the hill. While Minook went up the hill for another load, Erinia brought the furs back into the storeroom, trying to put them away the way they had been stored, but she wasn't tall enough or strong enough to lift the bundles of marten up to their hooks. She had been feeling so good about being big enough to carry the furs to safety, but she wasn't big enough to put them away. Mamma came to the storeroom door and looked at the mess. Erinia wailed, "Oh, Mamma, I just can't do it!"

"Never mind," Mamma said, "We'll do it together. Lena will tidy up the kitchen. You just keep bringing the furs in here and I'll hang them up."

By the next day everything was back in order. The woodcutting tools were back in the wood yard, the forge was in its place, the boys brought all the things down from the watchtowers, and Mamma and Erinia had seen that the furs were carefully stored back in the fur room, not at all damaged.

After the high water the grass lakes were filled with runoff water and there were no blackfish in them, so they had no meat or fish at all to eat. The flour was gone. They had oat groats and tea, and sugar, dried peas, and lard, and some hardtack. There were still some berries from last summer and some canned peaches, and that was all. They certainly would not starve, but it was bad that they were out of flour.

Mamma set Erinia to grinding the oats in the big grinder to make a sort of flour for bread. The oat flour baked into a pale loaf, not nearly as good Mamma's black

Russian bread made of rye flour, but it was some kind of bread, and that was better than none. There was lard to put on the bread, and that made the oat bread taste better, but they all longed for meat and fish. Still, they wouldn't have to eat babiche.

Erinia was fretting about Stepan and Papa, who hadn't taken much food with them. Certainly not enough to last so long. When she saw Mikhail chopping wood in the yard, she ran to tell him her worry.

"Probably they got a caribou, and probably they stopped to make dry meat out of it," he said. "Don't worry."

Erinia could think of a dozen kinds of trouble Papa and Stepan had met. They could have been eaten by a bear. A mean, hungry spring bear. They could have broken their legs. Perhaps they had lost their food or their flints to make a fire. Maybe it was cold in the hills where they went, and maybe they'd frozen their feet in the overflow. Maybe they'd gone snow-blind. But no one would talk to her about it. They just said not to worry.

Erinia thought that Old Man Kozevnikoff seemed like half himself without Papa and that Mikhail looked like half himself without Stepan.

The boys were so quiet Erinia was sure they thought Papa and Stepan were dead. Mamma of course thought that, because she always expected the worst to happen, and was hard and silent.

The day after the high water dropped, Erinia found Old Man Kozevnikoff in the store sitting on the bench by the stove, staring at the floor. He was holding his pipe as he usually did when he sat there, but there was no smoke, and Erinia could see that it was empty. "Do you want me to bring the tobacco for you?" she asked.

"No," he said. "No, I can't enjoy my pipe when I know Stepan and Ivan are out of tobacco."

"When will they come back?" asked Erinia.

Old Man Kozevnikoff bent to put a log in the stove.

"Oh, soon, soon," he said in a pretend-cheerful voice. He shut the door to the stove, fastened the clamp that pulled the door tight, and adjusted the damper. Then he straightened and looked at her, his face without expression. He shrugged, just a little, to say he didn't know. It was such a little shrug that Erinia knew he'd lost hope.

Erinia went to Papa's desk and sat on his high stool. There was Papa's perfect writing in the ledger book, all the graceful loops and thick and thin places, without a smear, without a blot. Suddenly hot tears were running down her cheeks. Oh, where were they? Why didn't they come?

Chapter Ten

A FEW MORNINGS LATER ERINIA CLIMBED OUT OF HER BED before anyone else was up. She dressed and went out to sit on the riverbank in the morning sun. There were no more big slabs of ice on the river, just flat cakes of ice from the sides of the river bumping into one another, turning in lazy circles on their way downriver. There was a pale green mist of new leaves on all the birch trees. The birds had come back from the places they'd been all winter, and the quiet woods were suddenly full of their songs. Erinia felt angry at the birds for sounding so happy. Didn't they know Papa and Stepan had not come back?

The dogs tethered by the edge of the bank were lying stretched out with their chins on their paws when suddenly they lifted their heads. They jumped to their feet and looked at the trail behind the odinochka in a pleased and expectant way, their tails wagging.

Then they began to bark their high, happy barks, and out of the woods came Papa and Stepan.

Erinia tried to shout, but nothing came out of her throat. She ran as fast as she could and threw herself so hard on Papa that he staggered and almost fell.

"My Erinia," said Papa in a funny voice. "Did you think we were lost?" Erinia took Papa's rough hand and then reached for Stepan. She couldn't speak.

The others had known what the dogs' barking meant, and in minutes there was Lena, still in her funny long nightgown, hugging Stepan and Papa, and the boys and Mikhail, all tousled with sleep, and Mamma, with tears in her eyes, stroking Papa's arm. Old Man Kozevnikoff kissed Papa and Stepan on both cheeks at least a dozen times, nearly pulling them off their feet with his enthusiasm.

Of course Papa and Stepan were very hungry, and soon they were all together around the table in the store, except for Old Man Kozevnikoff, who was too pleased and relieved to sit still. He bounded around the room making loud and boisterous jokes about the terrible shaggy beards that Stepan and Papa had grown, their dirty clothes and muddy faces.

Lena clucked over their thinness, and she and Mamma

brought all the food they could find to set on the table. Stepan sighed happily over the funny pale oat bread they'd made.

"I missed bread," he said.

Papa and Stepan drank cups and cups of tea. Mamma had to fill the samovar again before breakfast was over. Erinia was glad that at least there was still tea and lots of sugar.

"I missed tea," said Stepan.

Erinia stayed pressed to Papa's side as if she was afraid he'd disappear if she moved. Minook and Pitka went out to fire up the bathhouse so Papa and Stepan could get clean, and when they had finished eating, Old Man Kozevnikoff brought out the tobacco. Papa and Stepan were very pleased to be smoking their pipes again, and so was Old Man Kozevnikoff.

"I misssed my pipe more than I missed bread or tea," said Stepan. When at last Papa and Stepan had been to the bathhouse and had shaved and put on clean clothes, Old Man Kozevnikoff couldn't wait any longer to hear everything that had happened to them.

"Now," he said, "tell us why you were so late."

"You thought we would not come back, didn't you!" Papa said, smiling his biggest smile.

"No, no," Mikhail said. "Not for a minute!"

Old Man Kozevnikoff made low noises in his throat to

show how he had not worried a bit, and even Pitka and Minook and Elia shrugged to show their unconcern.

"We knew you were not in trouble. Good woodsmen like yourselves. We never worried," said Elia.

Erinia looked at them in surprise. She knew very well that they had been worried. So did Mamma and Lena, because they both stared at the men and gave little humphs to show what they thought.

"After we left," said Stepan, "did it get warm very suddenly? Really warm, everything melting fast?"

"No," said Old Man Kozevnikoff. "Nothing unusual. Soft snow during the day, hard crust on it at night."

"Ice in the puddles in the morning," said Pitka.

"Well," said Stepan, "we didn't have any ice in our puddles. As soon as we reached the hills, it warmed up so much all that snow got rotten. I never saw such weather. The snow was very deep to begin with, up there by the hills, deeper than we had here. We couldn't even walk with snowshoes, the snow was so deep and soft, half water. And at night it wasn't much better. No crust at all. So we knew we were in trouble. We'd have to stop and camp until the snow was gone. Not a chance to travel on that slush, and not a chance for any hunting."

Papa nodded. "We were by a nice little lake there, already half thawed. There were some muskrat. We got some with the bow, and there were some blackfish swimming in the water on top of the ice we could just grab with our hands. Not a lot to eat, but something. We rationed our tobacco. One pipe a day."

"That was hard," said Stepan. "When you don't have much to do, you want your pipe."

"But there was a lot more to worry about than soft snow," said Papa. "We were about a mile from a little river near the Yukon. That river must have jammed with ice, because the water in the lake and the creeks began to rise."

"Fast," said Stepan. "That water rushed so fast over the slush and snow it made a little whisper, like wind. At first we thought it *was* the wind."

"Edzegee," said Mamma with a shudder.

"We began to hike as fast as we could through that mushy snow to the highest place we could see, a little rise," said Papa. "Not even a hill. But there was a little stand of some young birch trees there. There weren't any branches big enough to stand on, and we didn't know what we'd do if the water came over the knoll. Finally we lashed our snowshoes up in the birches so we'd have a place to sit, and we hoisted our pack of food up and tied it to a high branch. We'd saved some of the muskrat, and we had most of Mamma's dry meat. We weren't going to starve, but we might get hungry.

"That water was so cold and so black. It crept up our

little knoll, and soon our trees were in the water and we had to climb onto our snowshoe perch. We wished we had two more pairs of snowshoes. There was floodwater as far as we could see. We could see a mamma bear with her new cub in a treetop about half a mile away."

"And there we were," said Stepan. "Nothing to do but sleep and wake up and sleep some more."

"Papa, how did you keep from falling into the water when you went to sleep?" asked Erinia.

Papa showed with his hands how they'd arranged the snowshoes. "We each were sitting on a snowshoe, with our legs wrapped around the tree trunk. The other snow-shoe was lashed up higher on the trunk so we could lean against that. We could hang our arms over that snowshoe and sleep that way. We didn't both sleep at once. Stepan kept watch when I was sleeping, and if he saw me slump-ing down toward the water, he'd yell and hit me with a birch switch to wake me up. We got cold because our clothes were damp and because we weren't moving much. In the day the sun would warm us for a little while, but at night we were really cold."

"I would go crazy stuck in a tree," said Mikhail.

"No," said Papa. "It wasn't so bad. We told each other stories, and then we watched the sky. I never noticed lots of things about the sky, different kinds of clouds, all the different colors in the morning and at night, the geese and ducks flying past all day long." Papa stopped for a moment and looked as if he was seeing that sky again.

"And then on the third night we both fell asleep, and when we woke up, the water was all gone and there was a thick layer of muck everywhere. The water went down as fast as it had come up."

"I'm sorry I missed it," said Stepan. "I would have liked to see that water run away, run backward!"

"And then we came home. We had to get across the mudflats with our snowshoes. It was slow going. And it didn't do the snowshoes any good. We have to get busy and make some new ones now."

"What happened to the mamma bear and her baby?" asked Erinia.

"Oh, they were gone from their tree by the time we woke up that morning," said Stepan. "They must have been a lot hungrier than we were."

Papa and Stepan slept the rest of that day and all night as well. Erinia tiptoed around in the store and listened outside their doors. She listened to Stepan's terrible snoring and felt like laughing and crying at the same time. Now everything was right again.

The next day Stepan and Papa walked with her down to the river and stared at the high-water mark left behind by the muddy river. They both shook their heads. It had been so close, the big flood. "But not *this* year," said Stepan.

For all the trouble they'd had, Papa and Stepan hadn't seen any big game, or any small game either, so they were all still hungry for meat.

Pitka and Elia took their canoes across the river to the flats to hunt ducks and geese. Erinia begged to go, but they said it was too dangerous with the ice still in the river. They were very lucky and came back with four fat ducks.

Mamma sent Erinia to pluck off the feathers. This had to be done a long way from the house. Too close was hutlaanee. Then Mamma gutted the ducks and carefully saved the fat from the intestines in a birch-bark basket. She was very pleased to have it because that was the very best grease for cooking, she said.

Mamma made a wonderful soup from those ducks, with groats and new wild onions, and that soup made up for the lynx Erinia hadn't been able to eat.

One morning, when there was no more ice floating down the river, Elia came into Erinia's room before she was awake. He had on his traveling clothes. He sat on the edge of her bed and smiled at her.

"You must come and tell me good-bye, my little Erinia."

Erinia blinked at him. She hadn't known he was going anywhere. "Where are *you* going, Elia?"

"When the company men were here, they brought a message that I should come to Ikogmute. You remember they told us that the baidarshchik there died during the winter? The company asked me to take his place."

"Oh," said Erinia. Elia would be a baidarshchik like Old Man Kozevnikoff. For a second Erinia felt worried because Elia wasn't fat enough for the job.

Elia stroked her cheek. "I want you to remember when I'm gone not to do anything foolish. I won't be there to keep the ice from falling on you next time. Now, get dressed and come to say good-bye."

Erinia wanted to cry, so she frowned hard at the floor. She couldn't imagine life without Elia.

On the riverbank she buried her face in Papa's shirt and wouldn't look at Elia. He squatted down beside her and coaxed her. "Come on, Erinia, you wouldn't let me go without a good-bye. Your old friend Elia? Remember, you said my name first!"

Then she had to peek out at him and smile a little, but there was a terrible knot in her throat.

Then Elia put his rifle and pack into his canoe and climbed in after them. He picked up his paddle and smiled good-bye to them all. Then he pushed away from the bank, and his canoe was caught in the current and moved away downriver, as steady as a heartbeat.

Lena watched him go with tears streaming down her

face. He was a grown man, she said, and of course he could go off on his own, but they would miss him.

Erinia thought how hard it must be to be a mother and know you are raising your children just to go away from you. She would never go away from Mamma and Papa.

Chapter Eleven

WHEN THE RIVER WAS FREE OF ICE, THEY ALL HAD TO DO a dozen things to get ready for fishing: patch the canoes and fix the dip nets, make new fish traps and fishing spears. Mamma insisted that they must carve the spear points from caribou bone because it was hutlaanee to use any metal at all when you were fishing. Even a knife.

Mamma was very careful to see that the boys knew exactly how to do everything connected with fishing.

"When people look for a husband for their daughter, they look to see what skill a boy has at fishing," Mamma said. "Hunting can go badly for anyone. The animals might migrate or become scarce in hard winter. But the fish are always here and they are the most important food for everyone. So people look to see which boys build the best fish traps and can set them well."

Erinia knew that her brothers were very good at fishing, and it made her cross to think that there were mammas and papas who were watching them, wanting to take them away to be husbands for their daughters. Well, let them find husbands someplace else. They couldn't have *her* brothers.

One morning Erinia dashed into the kitchen to get her tea, and Mamma stopped her as soon as she stepped in the kitchen. "Kkaa!" barked Mamma. That meant, stop that running! And be careful. Mamma was making a new fishnet. While Erinia was sleeping, she'd strung the guidelines up across the length of the back kitchen wall. Erinia had to be careful not to run into it or she'd ruin Mamma's work. She'd done that once when she was little. She'd been all tangled in Mamma's net, and Mamma had been very angry at her.

Because of that Mamma was always nervous about her fishnet and scolded Erinia every time she came near the net. She didn't really want her in the kitchen until that net was finished, but she said Erinia had to learn, so she'd better watch. A woman had to be able to make fishnets or she'd be useless.

"But you'd better sit very still and not bounce or dance or do anything else," said Mamma sternly.

Mamma's old fishnet was made with willow bast, the insides of willows. This bast was dried, and then Mamma rolled it with her fingers into a long thread, adding more and more to it until it was so long it had to be wound on a spool. Bast nets rotted easily, so you had to take them out of the river every few days to dry thoroughly.

This new net was made of rabbit sinew, which was stronger and didn't rip so easily. The net was made with a bone shuttle, which Mamma wove in and out in a complicated pattern, and the net was rapidly growing longer.

Erinia watched and frowned and frowned and watched until her eyes ached, but it was no use. She'd never be able to make a net like Mamma did. And even if she could learn the pattern, she'd never have the patience to stand in one place for hours and weave the shuttle in and out, in and out.

Erinia worried that she was going to grow up to be useless.

Later, while Mamma worked on the fishnet, she sent Erinia out to the woods beyond the odinochka fence to dig spruce roots. Erinia was eight now, big enough to get them by herself, but she had to be very careful not to cut herself with the sharp knife Mamma gave her to cut the roots.

She had to be very careful of beaver sticks, places where the beavers had chewed small trees for their feed pile.

"The stumps are sharp and pointed, sticking up above

the snow, and they're dangerous to fall on. You must look for them when you see beaver signs," said Mamma.

Erinia had to get a lot of spruce roots. Mamma would split the long, thin roots, which would make a kind of strong cord used to decorate the tops of baskets and to tie everything that needed tying. It would be very bad to run out of spruce roots.

But none of the roots Erinia gathered would be used to tie fish traps or to make canoes. That was hutlaanee. Only men could gather the spruce roots that were used for that, Mamma said.

It was very hard work, but she wanted to get more than anyone else had ever gotten. She wanted everyone to say what a good job she'd done.

In the woods thick bushes of wild pink roses crowded the trees and the path. And by every bush grew masses of delicate bluebells with sturdy stems and leaves, as if the roses and bluebells were friends who had to do everything together. The sun shone through the new leaves, and all the spruce trees had bright new green tips on their branches.

The willow leaves had a silvery side and a green side, so that the leaves flashed in the breeze, now silver, now green.

Best of all Erinia loved the little aspen leaves, which were perfectly round and shimmered on the trees in the tiniest movement of air. Each kind of tree had its own leaf song, but Erinia thought those round leaves had the most beautiful song of all.

Trees made other sounds as well. Erinia liked to put her ear against a tree trunk and listen. When you did that, you could hear wonderful noises from inside the trees, just the way she could hear gurgling when she put her ear up against the belly of a puppy. Inside themselves the trees hummed and screaked and almost whistled. It was like listening to someone's secret thoughts. Trees were like people: they didn't show on the outside what they were thinking.

With a stick she dug in the cold earth under the trees until the damp roots were exposed. They looked like long, skinny fingers, and sometimes Erinia was almost afraid to cut them, as if they would let out a scream.

According to Mamma, there were special words to say in Athabascan to thank the spruce for their roots, but Erinia didn't know what they were.

It took her all afternoon to gather a big basketful. Mamma was pleased. "That's good, Erinia," said Mamma solemnly. "If you get as much tomorrow, we will have enough." Erinia ran with her full basket to show Papa and Old Man Kozevnikoff what she had done.

"Ah, Erinia," said Papa, "you are getting to be such a big girl. Soon someone will ask to marry you, and then who will work so hard for us?" Papa always teased her like that, but it made Erinia uneasy to think that someday she would have to leave Papa and Mamma. She just wouldn't, and that was that. She would stay and take care of them forever.

There was no end to the work in the spring. The old canoes were patched, but one was beyond repair, so Stepan was making a new one for himself. He did such slow and careful work shaping the birch pieces of the frame that Erinia grew impatient watching him. She liked to do things fast.

"When will you make a canoe for me?" Erinia asked.

He smiled. "You're getting to be a very big girl. Soon I'll make you one of your own." Then he scowled. "Not *too* soon, though. I can just imagine what trouble you could get into on that river."

It was women's work to sew the birch bark onto the frame with spruce roots and to fill the seams with pitch. When Stepan was finished with the frame, Mamma and Lena began to cover it. Mamma called Erinia over to see how it was done.

"Watch carefully, Erinia," said Mamma.

Mamma had taught Lena how to do it, because where Lena came from they made a different kind of canoe, a *baidarka* made of sealskins. A baidarka was covered even over the top, except for a round hole where the man would sit. If a big wave came and sloshed over the boat, the boat would stay dry inside and only the top half of the man would get wet.

Erinia thought that was a very good idea.

The first big, lazy spring mosquitoes had come out of their winter place under the bark of the spruce trees. Mamma and Lena were halfway through with the cover when Mamma said, "Erinia, make some smoke for us." Erinia had to keep a piece of shelf fungus burning on a piece of tin so the smoke would drive the mosquitoes away. Erinia sometimes thought the choking smoke that stung her eyes was worse than the mosquitoes.

While Mamma and Lena finished the canoe cover, Stepan got ready to paint it. He made paint from a special red rock they got up the Koyukuk River.

"Here," he said to Erinia. "Grind this rock into the tin and you can help me make the paint."

It was hard work grinding the rock against a big stone. Erinia was hot and sweaty and was feeling very cross when Stepan took the rock from her. He could grind much faster, and soon he had enough. Then he showed her how to mix the red rock dust with some fish oil, and that made a lovely paint. Erinia wished they could paint everything that bright, wonderful color.

When the paint had dried, the canoe had to be taken very carefully on its first trip. It was the Athabascan belief that if any harm came to the canoe on its first trip, it would lose its luck. Mamma tied some red beads and grass on the seat in the boat, and then she sang a special song to keep the canoe safe. She helped Stepan into the canoe and watched anxiously as he paddled away. Papa smiled at Mamma's worried face, but everyone tried to do as she asked to follow her customs even if they didn't believe in them.

When all the chores were done to get ready for the fishing, it was time to cut spruce poles. Spruce poles were used to make fishtrap fences and racks for the fish to dry on.

The poles had to be thin, so they used only the skinny young spruce trees. First Mikhail cut the spruce down, and then Stepan knocked all the little branches off with his Aleut hatchet.

They cut down more than fifty poles and dragged them to the riverbank. Erinia liked to work with Mikhail and Stepan, they were so good-natured, so she helped them strip the bark off the spruce poles.

The bark came off easily in little curling strips, and Erinia liked the smell of the wet yellow wood underneath the bark. Newly peeled spruce poles smelled as if they would be good to eat.

But pitch from the spruce blackened their hands and made them sticky, and it had to be scrubbed off with sand. Mamma warned her again and again about the pitch, but Erinia was careless and got some in her hair.

A lot of it.

The look on Mamma's face when she saw Erinia's hair was terrible, and Erinia wanted to run away.

"I don't see how it got there, Mamma," Erinia whispered. "I didn't put my hands in my hair. The pitch just jumped there somehow."

"Daalek!" said Mamma furiously. Be quiet!

Mamma and Lena untied Erinia's braids and tried to work the pitch out by rubbing sand through her hair, but it was no use.

There was nothing to be done but cut the pitch out of Erinia's hair. So with her tlaabaas Mamma sliced off Erinia's hair just below her ears.

Lena cried to see Erinia's hair cut off. A woman's hair was never cut, except to show grief over someone's death. Mamma's and Lena's hair hung below their knees when it was unbraided.

Minook and Pitka were very nice, but Erinia could see that they wanted to laugh at her short hair. She scowled hard at them so they wouldn't dare.

She herself thought it felt wonderful to have all of that hair off her back, off her neck. She felt free and wild as an animal without those long braids bouncing behind her, pulling at her scalp, tangling in the willows.

She was glad she got pitch in her hair.

Chapter Twelve

THE SUMMER LEAVES GREW HEAVY AND DARK AND GLOSSY, the grass was tall all along the lakes, and there were hot, hot days.

The dogs were shedding their heavy coats. Great hanks of their hair fell out, and they dug deep, cool holes to escape the hot sun and hide from the dreadful mosquitoes, which bit their tender noses and eyelids.

It was too hot for Erinia, too. The heat made her feel as lazy as the fluffs of cottonwood seeds that floated on the river. She remembered what it was like on a cold winter day, the snow so blue in the cold sun, and wished she had some of that coldness to hold close.

When the Kaiyuh people came back to the Yukon to

fish, Kkaabaa and some of the others made their birch-bark shelters on the bank by the odinochka. Other families went to good fishing places farther downriver.

It didn't take very long to make the little huts. After Kkaabaa made the spruce-pole frame, Erinia and Nilaat stitched together big pieces of birch bark and covered the frame with those, overlapping them to keep rain out of the stitch holes. And that was a summer house.

Every year the Kaiyuh people made a special cere-mony down on the beach for the first salmon caught. If a big salmon was the first fish they caught, that was bad luck. But this year it was a small salmon, and that meant that there would be a heavy run of fish, so everyone was very happy about that.

When the salmon came, everyone was very busy.

The men went out in their canoes twice a day to take the fish out of the nets and three times a day to check the fish traps.

Some of them stood in the cold water of the eddy and speared the fish or caught them up in dip nets.

The women had to do the rest of the work. On squares of rough bark they slit the fish down the middle and gutted them. Once the fish were hung on spruce-pole racks, it was Erinia and Nilaat's job to put a little stick inside each fish to hold the sides of the body open so it would dry quickly and not grow mold. Old Man Kozevnikoff had taught some of the people the Russian way to cut the fish down both sides so that it didn't have to be held open with a stick. But Mamma liked to do things the old way, the way she'd been taught. Erinia and Nilaat wished she would give the old ways up, because they were very tired of putting the sticks in the fish.

Lena salted and smoked some of their salmon in the Russian way, the way Papa and Old Man Kozevnikoff liked it. Papa said he would give up tobacco and tea for good smoked salmon, but Erinia was sure he was joking.

The first fish to come up the river, early in the summer, were king salmon. Next came the dog salmon and then the silver salmon. The dog salmon had very tough skin, so the women pulled the skins off carefully and rolled them up to save to sew with. Those skins would be used to make good waterproof boots and parkas.

Forest fires began as usual during the dog salmon run. A strong smell of smoke came from a fire far, far across the river in the hills, and through the haze of smoke the sun looked like a throbbing orange ball. Sometimes the smoke was so thick that Erinia's and Nilaat's eyes stung.

But the good thing about the smoke was that there were no mosquitoes to bother them.

∞

In the early fall the squirrels began frantically to throw pinecones from the very tops of the tallest spruce trees. Every year Erinia thought they behaved as if they'd forgotten that they must gather pinecones. Then suddenly they remembered and they hurried to make up for lost time.

The berries had become ripe, and Mamma asked Kkaabaa if Nilaat could come with them to pick. Kkaabaa grumbled, but Mamma knew she would say yes, because then she would have the berries Nilaat picked.

On a gray day, when the sky was full of low, tattered clouds, Erinia, Nilaat, Mamma, and Lena went across the wide river to the flats in Mamma's long canoe. Every open space along the banks was choked with purple and yellow wildflowers and tall magenta fireweed, and fields of delicate pink grass rippled in the little wind.

Mamma paddled, and Erinia and Nilaat trailed their hands in the cold brown river and watched the patterns the water made around their fingers.

"Look, it's like a dance," said Erinia. "It makes the same pattern over and over until you change the position of your fingers. A water dance."

Lena sat in the front of the canoe and used the long pole to push them along when they got close to the bank, where the water was shallow.

The tundra that stretched before them smelled wonderfully of spruce and berry bushes and Labrador tea, sharp smells that made the inside of your nose prickle.

As soon as they got out of the canoe, the mosquitoes found them. Mamma and Lena gave the girls cotton scarves to cover their heads, but still the swarms whined around them, biting their hands and faces. There was nothing to be done about it, so they tried not to think of them, but as they fixed their scarves they contorted their mouths in horrible ways to blow air up into their faces to chase away the mosquitoes.

Erinia and Nilaat tried to see which of them could make the most horrible mosquito-blowing face, but Mamma frowned at them. "Kkaa!" That meant to stop fooling around and pick berries.

Mamma and Lena began to pick right there, but Nilaat and Erinia went farther out into the tundra, near the little spruce trees that edged the creek.

Nilaat was the sort of picker who squatted down and stripped every berry off her bush.

Erinia was the sort who grew impatient with the bush she was working on because she was always sure there was another, better bush nearby, with much larger berries.

When Erinia would call out, "Nilaat! Come and see how big the berries are on this bush!" Nilaat would just smile and cry, "When I've finished this bush!"

Nilaat was also the sort of picker who didn't take leaves off with the berries. Her basket of berries was as clean as could be. But Erinia's berries were full of twigs and leaves, and Mamma would scold her.

Sometimes Erinia stopped picking berries just to admire them. Then Nilaat would look up at Erinia with a smile and shake her head. But blueberries had a little star at the bottom of the berry, where the blossom had been, and they were covered with a blue, powdery frost that Erinia liked to erase with her thumb so she could see the tight, shiny, dark skin underneath.

And blueberries weren't blue inside, but a beautiful pink-purple. She wondered if Nilaat had ever noticed that, but she decided not to ask.

Everything on the tundra was beautiful. The Labrador tea and the blueberry leaves were tipped with orange and scarlet, and the soft, spongy moss had already turned yellow.

When you put your face down close to the ground, the tundra plants were like the smallest imaginable world, a miniature woods full of strange and wonderful trees and flowers: stiff gray lichen with ruffled edges and red lichen that clung to the rocks; threadlike flower stalks with red flowers the size of a bead; tiny, tiny white mushrooms; glossy leaves with clusters of polished black berries. A pale yellow spider scuttled through the black berries.

"Look, Nilaat. What would it be like to be that spider, taking a walk through the tall, tall lichen trees, stopping to look at the red flowers? Maybe there are little, little berries for him to pick, so small we can't even see them!"

Nilaat just laughed when Erinia talked this way. She said she didn't know how Erinia got ideas like that. Erinia didn't know either.

When they'd filled a basket, they would take it back to the canoe and get another basket to fill. They had to walk very carefully going to the canoe, for the big tussocks of grass rolled under their feet and made them stumble, and they could spill their berries.

Nilaat filled her baskets faster than Erinia did, but Erinia would get an empty basket at the same time anyway.

Nilaat's last basket was filled to the top and Erinia's was almost full when a brown-nosed black bear suddenly rose up out of the bushes nearby, standing tall on his hind legs. They hadn't heard him and he hadn't heard them, so they were all surprised.

He sniffed the air and stared at them with his little, nearsighted eyes, trying to see what kind of animals they were.

Erinia's heart started to beat so hard she felt it knocking against her ribs, and then she could hear it throbbing in her ears.

"Don't run," she said to Nilaat, her voice shaking. That was the only thing she could remember from the bear warnings everyone had given her since she was a baby.

Nilaat bent, carefully keeping her eyes on the bear,

and put her berry basket on the ground in front of her. "Put your basket down. Give him your berries," said Nilaat.

Erinia thought about how hard she'd worked for those berries. "No," she said, and gripped her basket more tightly.

Erinia and Nilaat began to walk backward, keeping an eye on the bear, talking soothingly to him.

"Good bear, nice bear, eat the berries. Good bear, good bear."

The bear didn't seem to notice Nilaat's berries. He lightly lowered himself on his four paws again and then went back to eating berries from the bushes.

When they'd put a good distance between the bear and themselves, they began to walk faster, still looking over their shoulders until they came to Mamma and Lena.

"Mamma, a big animal," said Erinia, because she knew that in the Indian way it was hutlaanee to say the bear's name.

Mamma looked back at the place where the bear was and called to Lena, who was picking farther away in the tundra. "Lena, we'll go now," she said, and pointed to the bear. They all walked quietly to the canoe. They put their baskets with the others in the bottom of the canoe, and Lena poled the canoe out of the shallows.

"Oh," said Nilaat sorrowfully. "My beautiful berries."

"Never mind that," said Mamma. "It was a very smart thing to do, giving him your berries. You can have some of ours to make up for it. We have lots."

And they did. The bottom of the canoe was full of baskets heaped with berries, and there would be plenty for everyone.

Erinia was very glad Mamma didn't ask her why she hadn't given the bear *her* berries.

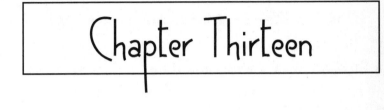

Chapter Thirteen

LATE THAT FALL, WHEN THE LEAVES HAD TURNED YELLOW, the Russian American Company sent three freight canoes from Saint Michael to buy dried fish from the Indians. The company had a lot of dogs to feed during the winter.

One of the company men was Yuri, who had never been to Nulato before. Erinia and Nilaat had never seen anyone like Yuri, so at first they were shy and peeked at him from behind the doors.

Yuri walked with a bounce, and he laughed with his head thrown back and his white teeth flashing. He was almost as loud as Old Man Kozevnikoff and just as joyful.

Yuri spoke languages they'd never heard, and when he

spoke to them in Russian, he pronounced his words differently than they did.

"Papa," said Erinia. "What kind of person is Yuri?"

Papa smiled at Erinia. "Until a few years ago there was a Russian fort in a warm place called California. It's so warm there it never snows, and that's where Yuri came from."

Erinia hadn't known there were places without snow.

"Do they have rain, Papa?"

Papa laughed. "Oh, yes. I think there is no place without rain. They grew vegetables and fruit and wheat and beef in California to ship to New Arkhangel. I often saw these people from Fort Ross when I was a boy. Yuri is a creole. His mother was a California Indian, so Yuri speaks her language, of course."

Sometimes Yuri would speak Spanish for them. "*Gracias,*" said Yuri when Erinia brought him tea. "*Buenos días,*" he said in the morning. Erinia thought Spanish was the most beautiful language she'd ever heard. Athabascan was harsh in the throat and full of sharp edges, and Russian thudded and pounded, but Spanish was silky and smooth and gentle.

Yuri was soon in the middle of the fishing camp, talking away with everyone who could speak Russian and making signs to those who couldn't.

Yuri could do many things they'd never heard of. He

had worked with cattle on a ranch in South America, and he knew how to use a rope so that it would rise above his head in a quivering, lazy circle and then come down, *plop*, on whatever Yuri'd set his eye on. One of the dogs got loose while they were loading fish into the canoes, and Yuri caught that dog in the loop of the rope.

Everyone wanted to learn right away how to do that, but no one could make even one loop. Yuri said it took a lot of practice.

But that wasn't even the best thing Yuri could do.

He had brought his fiddle with him. Yuri said that was its English name, and he told them the name in Russian and Spanish as well. But Erinia thought fiddle was a perfect name because that was the sound it made, *fiddlefiddlefiddle*, when Yuri played it fast.

A fiddle had strings, but it wasn't the same shape as Lev's balalaika, and it had four strings instead of three. And it was played with a bow, which was just like the bow on a fire drill, except that it had strings on it.

A fiddle could make lots of different sounds, sorrowful and sweet and best of all, merry.

Every night in the big yard of the odinochka Yuri would sit on the spruce stump the boys used for splitting wood, and he'd play songs he'd learned in California.

Everyone from the fish camp came to listen and stomp their feet. He played "The Yellow Rose of Texas" and

"The Bonnie Blue Flag" and "Oh, Susanna" and "Dixie" and many others that Erinia didn't learn the names of. Yuri's songs were just like the music Lev played for the Cossack dances. No one could sit still.

When he saw how much everyone liked his music, Yuri said he would teach everyone to do the square dance.

Erinia was very glad about that. Some kinds of music had to have dancing to go with them. Otherwise there was nothing for you to do with all that feeling that was in your feet, and the rest of you.

Yuri had everyone line up in the dirt in front of the store, and then he patiently taught them what to do when he called out the instructions: promenade, and allemande left, allemande right, and do-si-do and swing your partner. Erinia and Nilaat started out together as partners, but somehow it all got mixed up and Erinia was dancing with the old man who had the beaver-tooth tool, and Nilaat was with Pitka.

Soon everyone was dancing: the old people and the people in the middle who weren't young or old, the young men and women, the boys and girls, Papa and Mamma and Old Man Kozevnikoff and Lena and the boys. Erinia thought if old Simaaga had been there, he would have danced too.

The tops of the tall spruce trees around the odinochka turned gold in the late-evening sun, and Yuri's fiddle, held up high under his chin, flashed gold, and the thin dust they kicked up in the yard was golden too.

Deetza had her baby on her back, and every time she spun around with her partner, the baby would let out such a long, piercing, gleeful screech that everyone stopped dancing and doubled over, weak with laughter. Then the baby looked at them all with such astonishment that they had to laugh again.

It was the most fun any of them had ever had.

They were all very sorry when Yuri and the other company men had to take the fish down to Saint Michael, but Yuri said he'd be coming back to Nulato soon and then they could dance again.

Erinia changed her mind about getting married and thought that she wouldn't mind after all.

She'd marry Yuri when she was grown up, and she could dance and sing every night.

PART TWO

The Telegraph Men

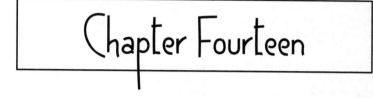

Chapter Fourteen

TWO SUMMERS PASSED, AND TWO MORE WINTERS. YURI came to fiddle in the fall, Lev and Dimitri and Nikolai came with the summer and winter provisions, and the Kaiyuh people came and went as they always did. Erinia liked the way things went around in a circle, over and over. It was something you could count on, the sameness.

Until the cold morning when the telegraph men came.

In the darkest part of winter they all went to bed earlier and slept later than they did at other times of the year. Erinia was allowed to sleep as long as she liked, so she was very surprised when Mamma shook her awake.

She sat up in bed, frightened by Mamma's urgency.

There was new frost on the log walls by her bed.

"*Edzoo!*" Erinia said. It's cold.

Mamma threw her clothes on the bed.

"Never mind that," said Mamma. "Get dressed and help with breakfast. We have visitors."

Erinia pulled on her calico dress and her apron. She tied her moccasins as fast as she could and ran to the kitchen.

Mamma was very excited, running here and there to boil salt fish and start the samovar. She took four black loaves from the shelf and told Erinia to put them on the big table in the store.

"And come right back for the lard," she said.

"Who came, Mamma?" Erinia asked. Mamma stopped for a minute to look at her.

"*Belakana,*" she said with wide eyes.

Americans.

Erinia stared back at her. They'd heard of Americans but never expected to see any on the river. And certainly not in the middle of winter.

Erinia made a basket of her apron and piled the loaves in. Then she ran into the store to see the Americans. But there she found only their old friend Ivan Lukin, smoking his pipe. Lukin was famous, the chief explorer for the company. He was a creole and he spoke dozens of languages—

the Russian of his father and the language of his mother, the two Eskimo languages, and nearly all the many kinds of Athabascan—so he was very valuable to the company. Erinia knew he came to Nulato only when something important was going on.

"Lukin, did you come with the Americans?"

"Yes, little Erinia." He smiled at her and reached over to pinch her cheek. "Not so little anymore. The last time I saw you, you had lost most of your teeth, and now they're all grown back!"

"Well, I'm ten now," said Erinia primly.

Lukin smiled and pointed at a place in his mouth where a tooth was missing. "I wish I could grow another tooth," he said.

"Lukin, why did you bring these Americans?" asked Erinia.

"The company has sent me to take care of them because they're new to this country and don't know anything. The head of the Russian American Company sent a letter saying that we are to treat them as our friends."

"Are they nice?" asked Erinia.

"Right now they're half frozen," said Lukin. "Their army coats and boots are not good enough for this cold weather. They have to get some native clothes or they won't last long."

At last Papa and Old Man Kozevnikoff came in from

the barracks with the four Americans. Minook and Pitka and Mikhail and Stepan, coming right behind them, were so excited that they all tried to squeeze through the door at the same time.

The Americans were wearing beautiful blue uniforms with gold lace trim. Little red cords ran down the pant legs, and shining brass buttons marched all down the front of the uniforms. The gold lace shimmered by the light of the petroleum lamps.

Erinia had never seen anything so splendid as those soldier uniforms.

Papa picked up Erinia's hand and said to the men in English, "This is my youngest daughter, Erinia Pavaloff."

She looked at Papa in surprise. She hadn't known he could speak English.

One of the soldiers had fine yellow hair that fell over his forehead. That hair looked so soft Erinia wanted to touch it.

The tallest soldier bent from the waist and took her hand and bent low over it. "Miss Pavaloff," he said. "George Adams at your service, ma'am."

She frowned hard. She didn't know what the words meant, but maybe he was making fun of her.

But then he smiled and she knew he wasn't.

She could see that he had frostbitten his face on the long trip. She pointed to his face and told him in Russian that he'd frozen his cheeks.

The soldiers looked at one another and laughed. They said something in English, and Papa said it meant "Such a little girl to speak Russian." That seemed a very odd thing to say, so Papa explained, "They're used to little girls who speak English, you see."

Another soldier had hair as dark as Erinia's, but his was thick and close to his head, in tight little curls like the wood shavings they made with the knife for fire starter. Erinia wanted to touch his hair too. His name was Lt. Fred Smith. The soldier with yellow hair was Lt. Sam Dyer, and the older man was the major. Major Kennicott, which sounded like an Indian name to Erinia. He was the leader of all of them.

Papa gestured to the table and told them in English to sit down. Then Old Man Kozevnikoff and Erinia brought them cups of tea from the samovar.

When Mamma came in with a tray of fish and the lard Erinia had forgotten, the soldiers all stood up from the table so suddenly that Mamma threw them a startled glance. The soldiers nodded politely as Papa introduced Mamma, and then they all sat down again just as suddenly. Erinia thought that standing up must be some sort of American custom. Mamma kept her eyes lowered and didn't look at the soldiers again while she put the food on the table. She was always frightened of strangers.

Pitka wanted Lukin and Papa to ask the soldiers about

their trip, but Lukin said, "Let them eat first. They're very hungry and very tired."

The dark-haired Lieutenant Smith ate as if he didn't want to waste time chewing. At last he turned to Lukin and Papa and spoke very emotionally in English, waving his arms about.

Lukin laughed and turned to Mamma. He told her in Athabascan, "The lieutenant says to tell you he has never before eaten such a wonderful meal."

Mamma smiled then and glanced at the young soldier. *Fish and bread and tea are not so wonderful*, Erinia thought. *These soldiers must have been very hungry on the trail.*

Soon everything on the table was gone but one small hunk of bread. Then the soldiers drank cups and cups of tea with lots of sugar. But still, they didn't drink as much tea as Papa and Old Man Kozevnikoff and Lukin.

Papa and Old Man Kozevnikoff lit their pipes and offered some tobacco to the Americans, but the soldiers took their own tobacco out of some small pouches and carefully pinched the tobacco into an oblong paper. They rolled that paper up into a thin tube and sealed it shut somehow, licking it all along the side, and when they'd put that tube in their mouth and lit it, it sent off smoke just like Papa's and Old Man Kozevnikoff's pipes. Everyone watched them intently. They'd never seen tobacco used like that before.

"Cigarettes," said George when he noticed that everyone was watching them.

"Cigarettes," said Old Man Kozevnikoff thoughtfully.

Papa explained why the soldiers had come to Nulato.

The Western Union Telegraph Expedition would build a telegraph line from Nulato to the Bering Strait, and then that line would be connected to a telegraph line being built in Russian Siberia and then to one being built in Canada.

Papa and Old Man Kozevnikoff were very excited about that.

"Imagine, people can send messages to each other by wires, they can talk to people they can't see! A message from the czar in Russia could come here to Nulato through the telegraph. In minutes!" It didn't seem possible.

But first they needed the right clothes. Many other telegraph men had stayed behind in Saint Michael, but Lukin said they would soon be coming to Nulato too.

They would need caribou parkas with wolf-lined hoods, thick mittens of wolf or beaver fur, pants made of hide with the fur turned in, and sturdy caribou moccasins with lots of room for straw and fur socks inside. And for the summer they would need fish-gut parkas to keep the rain off and waterproof sealskin boots.

So as soon as they were able to buy the clothes they needed from people at Saint Michael, they would never wear those useless uniforms again.

Erinia thought *that* was too bad.

And then, when they were properly dressed, they would start to survey the trail for the telegraph line.

Lukin took a letter out of his oilskin pouch and handed it to Old Man Kozevnikoff. "I almost forgot," he said. "I saw Elia in Ikogmute, and he gave me this."

Old Man Kozevnikoff beamed. "Go tell Lena to come!" he said to Erinia. So she ran to the Kozevnikoffs' rooms and came back pulling a pink-faced Lena by the hand. Old Man Kozevnikoff couldn't read, so he gave the letter to Papa to read out loud.

Elia's letter said he was well and enjoyed his work. He often saw Kate, who was also well and who sent her love to them. He had married a girl from a nearby village, a half-Russian girl named Fedosia, and he would bring her to visit when he could. She and Kate were good friends already, he said. Fedosia could sew and was very good-natured, he said. Like Mamma, he said. When Papa read that part, he looked up at Lena and smiled, and Lena hid her face in her hands, she was so pleased. Stepan and Mikhail and the boys cheered and laughed to think of Elia married.

Erinia made a sour face. Thinking of her Elia married made her feel cross.

Old Man Kozevnikoff and Lena couldn't stop smiling, talking to each other so fast in Aleut that their words seemed to tumble over one another. They spoke in Aleut only when they were very excited, because it seemed to them rude to speak in a language no one else understood. Papa explained to the Americans what the letter said.

"My daughter Kate is a student at the mission school at Ikogmute," he said. "She has been gone for three years. Long years," said Papa sadly. "And Elia is the Kozevnikoffs' son, a good boy, strong and hardworking, raised here with all my children. We've missed him very much while he's been gone. His father and mother are very proud of him. And now he has found a wife."

Old Man Kozevnikoff turned to them.

"Lena is now thinking of all the fat babies Elia will be bringing here to visit!"

Papa laughed, and when he told the soldiers what Old Man Kozevnikoff had said, they laughed too.

"Just like my mother," the major said.

The Americans were to stay in the big barracks with Mikhail and Pitka and the boys.

At night Mamma and Erinia took the men some caribou robes they could use for their beds.

They saw that the telegraph men had hung an American flag on the barracks wall, and next to it they had hung a painting of a man with a beard.

Erinia and Mamma looked at the picture for a moment.

"Kuklaa," said Mamma. Poor thing. Erinia knew she'd said that because the man in the picture looked so sad.

They had never seen any painting of a person before, except for the little icon Mamma had been given by Father Netsvetov when she was baptized.

"Is he a god?" Erinia asked. Stepan could speak a little English, so he asked the telegraph men why they had this man's picture on the wall.

The men were very eager to answer the question, and three or four of them were talking so fast and on top of one another that Erinia could tell Stepan was a little confused.

At last Stepan turned to Mamma and said in Russian, "His name is Abrimov Link, and he was the leader of the Americans. Like the czar of Russia, or Baranov at Sitka. He is sad because there was a great war in his country."

Some of the men began to talk fast to Stepan again. He listened, and then he turned to Erinia and Mamma.

"Abrimov Link was killed. This year a bad person shot him with a gun." Mamma nodded and sighed. There was so much trouble in the world. She put the robes on the table and pointed toward the store.

"Tsaaye," she said. That meant that the tea was ready if they wanted some.

Chapter Fifteen

LUKIN LEFT THE NEXT DAY TO GO BACK TO SAINT MICHAEL, and a few weeks later he brought more telegraph men. They were properly dressed in good Eskimo clothes, and they'd brought clothing for George and Fred and the other two men as well. The newcomers laughed at poor George, whose cheeks had turned black where they had been frozen.

The first supplies of food for the telegraph men came from Saint Michael soon after. Erinia poked and pried into the boxes and barrels until Mamma said, "Erinia, don't be a nuisance!"

She didn't want to be a nuisance, but she was nearly wild with curiosity. She'd never imagined that there were so many different things to eat.

Even though it looked like a lot of food, the telegraph men said it wasn't enough to last until the next shipment. They said the people in charge of the expedition did not ever send what they had been asked to send.

In the shipment there was a big barrel of strange-looking pale sauerkraut, which was supposed to keep the soldiers from having a disease called scurvy. But the sauerkraut had gone bad on the way to Saint Michael, and the men said they wouldn't eat it, even if they did get scurvy. That sauerkraut smelled so terrible that Erinia couldn't be in the same room with it.

They had meat she'd never heard of—barrels of salt pork, cans of beef and ham, and bacon. The soldiers cooked for themselves on the big stove in the store, and when they fried bacon, Erinia felt hungry right away. She couldn't imagine anything that could smell more delicious than bacon frying.

There were cans of red, squishy vegetables called tomatoes, which Erinia didn't think much of, and dried vegetables that were to be made into a soup. The best vegetables were little hard things called beans, which were very good when the telegraph men boiled them with the salt pork. But they had to boil them for a long time. One of the men, when it was his turn to cook, served them beans that were so hard they plinked against the tin plates.

There was a powder made of potatoes that tasted like nothing at all, but the men also had dried apples, which were cooked with sugar into a sort of mush that was delicious. There was a picture of apples on the box they came in. They looked like big red berries growing in a tree.

Erinia would like to see a tree like that someday.

The men liked to drink coffee more than they liked Russian tea. Coffee had a wonderful smell, but it didn't taste anything like it smelled, and after she tried it once, Erinia never wanted to try it again.

Pitka and Minook were not much interested in the strange food, but they were fascinated by the equipment the telegraph men had brought. The boys carefully examined their beautiful knives, the crowbars, and the picks and shovels that would be used to dig holes for the telegraph poles.

The soldiers' weapons made the boys' eyes shine. Minook and Pitka said they were much better than the old muskets everyone in Russian America used. They took apart the rifles and pistols and put them back together again and again to learn how they worked.

The telegraph men also had a thermometer to measure the coldness. They had surveying instruments, and maps and pens and beautiful handbooks with charts to change Russian measurements into American measurements, and maps of the stars in the sky.

They had a little thing with stiff bristles stuck into holes on a handle. Erinia brought it to Mamma. "Look," she said. She pretended to put the brush in her mouth and moved it back and forth. Mamma looked puzzled. "It's to keep your teeth clean," said Erinia. Mamma tucked the corners of her mouth in, which meant that she was not impressed, and Erinia wasn't either. "I think it would hurt your mouth to clean your teeth like that," she said.

The telegraph men had pocket watches to tell the time and compasses to show which way was north. Instead of wooden snow goggles they had spectacles with colored glass to keep from getting snow-blind, and things called scissors to cut things, which were like two knives fastened together.

Mamma was very interested in the scissors when she saw how quickly they cut through a piece of white cloth. George told her she could borrow them anytime.

Erinia didn't care much about the guns and tools and instruments. She just wanted to look at the photographs the telegraph men had. She had seen the painting of the American president, and Mamma's icon, but paintings didn't look real. Photographs looked so real you almost expected them to move at any moment.

No one at the odinochka had ever seen a photograph, though Papa and Old Man Kozevnikoff said they had heard of them when they visited Saint Michael. Erinia had never had any idea that such a thing existed.

Every day Erinia asked to look at the photographs again.

She could look at them for hours, asking dozens of questions about this person and that. Why did they all wear such fancy clothes, and why did they look so serious? What was this one's name, and how old was she, and could she sew?

Mamma was frightened to think that you could catch someone like that, freeze them in time forever.

"Hutlaanee," she said.

But Erinia thought it was wonderful. If you had a picture of someone, you could have them with you always, even if they were far away. Even if they were dead.

Papa and Old Man Kozevnikoff liked the white canvas tents the expedition had supplied, which were much lighter to carry in a sled than a caribou- or moose-hide tent. If the canvas tent got wet, it could easily dry in the sun, and light came through the fabric so that it wasn't dark in the tent.

And Papa and Old Man Kozevnikoff were very pleased with matches, little sticks that made fire when you rubbed them fast on something. A match was faster than flint, a flint was faster than a fire drill. Everything got faster and faster, Erinia thought. She tried to imagine a thing faster than a match, but she couldn't.

At night the telegraph men told them about the terrible American war that had just ended, and about other new things that were out in the world, like steam engines, which could carry long wagons along an iron trail, and instruments that would let you look closely at the faraway stars and at tiny things that were too small to see with your eyes.

Papa and Old Man Kozevnikoff were so hungry for the news that sometimes when the telegraph men were going yawning off to the barracks to sleep, they would follow them, pipes in hand, still asking questions.

The telegraph men taught Minook and Pitka to measure with their instruments. They measured the width of the Yukon in front of the odinochka. It was a mile and a quarter, they said. That was about two versts in the Russian way.

They had a book of maps of the world. Erinia wanted to see Russia first. It made her very proud that Russia was so big. This big country was her country and she was a Russian.

And there were the cities she'd heard about from Papa and Old Man Kozevnikoff—Saint Petersburg, where the czar lived, and Moscow, and Kamchatka, where Papa's father had been born.

She was sure Russia was very beautiful.

Erinia and Pitka and Minook studied the map of each country in the book. They couldn't read English, so the telegraph men told them the names of each country.

There was one page that showed both sides of the earth. The earth wasn't really flat like that, but round. The map was just laid out flat so it could be put in a book. You could get a round map too, which was called a globe. George said he'd had one in his home when he was a little boy. Erinia wanted very much to see a round globe.

Papa shook his head at the way the map had changed since he had gone to school in New Arkhangel. There had been so many wars, and the wars had changed the shapes of countries and the names, too, since he had been a boy. Erinia was surprised at that. She'd thought countries were forever, not things that could be changed.

Mamma got quieter and quieter as time went on. Erinia knew that since the telegraph men had come, Pitka and Minook did not listen patiently anymore when Mamma talked about the old ways. They were just too interested in the new ways.

They all had a good time learning each other's language. *"Kak eto budet parusski?"* the telegraph men would say, pointing to some object. What is that in Russian? Or they'd ask for a word in Athabascan because they said they needed to be able to speak to the people they came across while they were working on the telegraph line.

When Papa explained that the language spoken around Nulato was just one of the Athabascan languages, and that they'd need to speak Ingalik Athabascan when they got closer to the ocean, and two other kinds of Athabascan if they went upriver, the telegraph men decided to concentrate on Russian. Papa said nearly everyone they met would speak a little Russian.

Old Man Kozevnikoff and Papa would tell the telegraph men the word they asked for in Russian, and all the telegraph men would try to say it. Then everyone would laugh because the word always sounded funny the way they said it. George wrote all the words down in a notebook.

Then Erinia would ask for the English word for something and the soldiers would tell her, and when Erinia said it, that would sound funny too.

They laughed so hard it was a wonder they learned anything. But they did.

Papa had been taught English at school and he'd had to speak it often as a clerk, so he could talk to the "Boston men." That was what they called Americans in New Arkhangel. Of course he had spoken Russian and Tlingit as a child, and because a lot of Finns were working in New Arkhangel, he also spoke a little Finnish.

And when he came north, he'd learned Athabascan.

Five languages! The telegraph men were very amazed that such an ordinary man, a storekeeper, would be so learned. Erinia was amazed too. She hadn't known about the Finnish or the English.

The telegraph men asked Papa to say something in Tlingit. Papa spoke a few words, which he said were a Tlingit greeting, but then he made a little face. "It's strange," he said, "but I've almost forgotten the language. There's no one to speak it with, so it's not in my head any-more. When I look for the word, some other language jumps in front of it."

Stepan spoke four languages and Mikhail spoke three.

Old Man Kozevnikoff knew six languages. Russian, of course, and his own Aleut language, which he and Lena spoke together, and two kinds of Athabascan. He'd been a long time as baidarshchik at the post at the mouth of the Yukon, where he'd had to learn to speak Yup'ik, one of the Eskimo languages. And now he was learning English, too.

Erinia thought people before she was born must have been very smart to have learned so many languages. Except the Americans, of course, because they spoke only their own language.

Pitka and Minook learned English very fast. They all learned from the Americans, except Mamma and Lena, who weren't interested.

Erinia got along fine with the bigger English words, but the little words gave her trouble. She could never remember the difference between *him* and *her* and *she* and *he*. And those little words that were stuck in the middle of everywhere were dreadful. She would say very clearly as Fred had taught her, "Good morning. Did you have good sleep?" But then they would all tell her that she must say, "Did you have *a* good sleep?" The next time Erinia was sure she was saying it correctly, but instead she said, "Good morning. Did you have *the* good sleep?" and she was corrected again. But she listened very carefully when they spoke, and learned when to use *the* and *a*, though she couldn't see the use of *an* at all.

Erinia was very proud of her English. Soon she would be able to say she spoke three languages, which was not as much as Papa and Old Man Kozevnikoff, of course.

But still.

Chapter Sixteen

ALL WINTER THE TELEGRAPH MEN WENT BACK AND FORTH from Saint Michael and Unalakleet, looking for the right place to put the telegraph lines, building camps along the telegraph route, bringing in supplies.

The men all took turns staying behind in the barracks to rest, three or four men at a time. It was very hard working out in the cold, and so the telegraph men liked to be at Nulato, where they were comfortable. Most of all they liked the Russian steam baths.

Every Saturday Old Man Kozevnikoff sent Mikhail or Stepan to start a fire in the bathhouse. There was a big open-hearth stove to heat the big rocks that were used to make steam.

Erinia went to the water hole in front of the odinochka to fill the water barrel for the steam bath. There had to be water to make steam, and then there had to be water so that people could rinse off. The barrel was lashed onto the water sled, and she could haul it there herself, but once she'd filled it with bucket after bucket of water, someone else had to pull it to the steam bath. It was too heavy for her when it was full.

Erinia didn't like filling the water barrel, but she remembered how cheerfully Nilaat had always done the hardest work, and she didn't complain.

There were two rooms in the bathhouse. You undressed in the little room. In the winter the walls of that room were thick with frost, and the door was so frosted you could hardly yank it open.

Then you went into the big room, where you sat naked on a platform against the back wall and waited for the steam.

After the big rocks were heated enough, the burning sticks of wood and the ashes from the fire were taken outdoors. Then water was thrown on the rocks, and the room filled immediately with thick, choking steam. In a few minutes everyone in the bathhouse would be turned bright red, like a salmon.

The men went first, and then after the rocks had heated again, it would be the women's turn.

Lena had been used to steam baths in the Aleutians, but Mamma thought steam baths were just for Eskimos, and it had taken a long time for her to get to like them.

In the old days Mamma's people and Lena's people in the Aleutians hadn't any soap. So they saved their urine in special baskets, and they used that for washing. Urine was also good for tanning skins and for curing snow blindness and lots of other things.

Erinia did not like the sound of that at all.

Papa and Old Man Kozevnikoff said that the Yup'iks didn't use any water in their baths. They just made the room so hot that everyone sweated themselves clean. He said that Yup'ik women didn't take sweat baths—just the men and boys.

And they said the Finns in New Arkhangel used to roll in the snow after the steam bath or jump into the icy water of the bay. Erinia frowned at them because she was sure that they weren't telling the truth about those Finns. Who would do such a crazy thing?

But with good Russian soap and Yukon water it was wonderful to get so clean all over every week, and she was glad she wasn't a Yup'ik girl.

Erinia could hardly wait for spring, when the Kaiyuh people would come again. They would be so amazed when they saw the telegraph men!

If only Erinia could persuade the men to take out their uniforms and put them on. Erinia wanted Nilaat to see what they had looked like the first night they came, in those wonderful blue uniforms with the red stripes on the pants. Without their uniforms they looked almost like ordinary people, especially now that their faces were all windburned.

And what would the Kaiyuh people think when they saw the matches and rifles and scissors and beans!

What Erinia hadn't expected was how curious the telegraph men would be about the Kaiyuh people. As soon as they heard the gunshots from far away, the Indian signal that they were coming, the telegraph men came out of the barracks and stood on the riverbank to watch the long line of them come. They asked Papa why the men didn't carry anything, and the women and children pulled the sleds and carried the bundles.

"That's the custom," said Papa. "The men say that their hands must be free in case of attack." The telegraph men didn't say anything to that, but Erinia thought they looked disapproving. She had always felt the same way herself, when she saw little Nilaat with her heavy pack and the red marks the tumpline had pressed across her forehead when she took the pack off her back.

When the Kaiyuh people came up the steep bank and found the strangers waiting for them at the top, they seemed hardly to know what to do. The first ones stopped on the bank and stared. Papa and Old Man Kozevnikoff hurried to explain to them that it was all right, that these men were friends, but the Kaiyuh people still looked at the telegraph men from the corners of their eyes. The children didn't laugh, but stared round-eyed from the tops of the sleds where they were riding. One of the young men ran back to tell the others behind them about the new men, so that when the others came up the bank, they were looking expectantly for the strangers.

When Simaaga came up the bank, he stopped and with his feet planted far apart he looked arrogantly at the soldiers. Papa took the telegraph men to meet Simaaga.

He explained that Simaaga was the medicine man and that they'd do well to treat him with respect. George asked Papa if he should give Simaaga a gift, and Papa said he thought it would be a good idea, so George took the bowie knife from the sheath on his belt and presented it to Simaaga with a little bow. Papa told Simaaga that the telegraph men wished to gather information and wished to be their friends. Simaaga nodded shortly and took the knife. He gave it a very satisfied glance before he turned away, and Erinia could see that the old man was very pleased with his present.

As always, Nilaat came up the bank in the last straggle of children. She shifted the pack she was carrying and set it down, and then she stared at the soldiers with great interest. "Who are these?" she asked Erinia. Erinia took Nilaat's hand and led her to Fred Smith.

"Nilaat," she said. Fred took Nilaat's hand and bent over it the way George Adams had done when he first met Erinia. Nilaat gave him a pleased smile and reached up to touch his dark curls. Erinia had often wanted to do that, but she hadn't dared.

When the Kaiyuh people had gone to the underground houses, Erinia turned to Papa. "Can I take the telegraph men to watch the hello dance? Will Simaaga be angry if there are strangers there?"

"I think," said Papa, "that Simaaga would be happy to have the opportunity to show off in front of strangers."

Old Man Kozevnikoff laughed and said he thought so too. And it must have been true, because in the dance Simaaga howled and jerked and made more terrible noises than Erinia had ever heard him make before, to impress the telegraph men.

Lukin brought two new men to join the telegraph men at Nulato, but these two weren't soldiers. Frederick Whymper was an artist who'd been sent with the telegraph men to draw pictures of Russian America. And Dall was a scientist who had been sent to collect things for a museum in America. A museum was a place where you could go to see things from all over the world, he said.

So every day while the Indians went about their work at the underground houses, Whymper's pen flew across his paper, making pictures of everything: Simaaga in his eagle down, dancing the hello dance; old Seyula making fire with his drill; the women hauling water from the water hole in the river ice. When the people got used to Whymper, they stopped what they were doing to watch him, sucking in their breath, as if he were working magic. Whymper asked Erinia to tell them not to pay any attention to him, to go about their work, because he couldn't draw them if they were just standing and looking over his shoulder.

Dall asked the Kaiyuh people questions, which Papa repeated to them in Athabascan. Dall carefully wrote down the answers in a fat black book. Erinia thought she had never heard anyone ask so many questions before. She'd thought no one asked more than she did.

He wanted to know everything about the way the people lived and about the things they carried with them. Erinia was pleased that Dall liked all the old things she liked, and she helped him by asking people to take this and that out of the carrying bags to show him. She asked old Seyula to show him the beaver-tooth tool and asked Kkaabaa to show him her stone lamp. In a few days Dall had made hundreds of sketches and had filled the fat black book with writing.

"What would I have done without you?" he said to Erinia. "I wouldn't have known what was hidden in all those bags if you hadn't asked the people to show me their tools!"

"They used to be cross with me because I was too curious," said Erinia.

"Curiosity makes a good scientist," he said, and Erinia was pleased because no one before had ever thought curiosity was a good thing.

Dall asked Mamma to explain all the things that were hutlaanee so he could write them in his book. Erinia's English was not good enough yet to explain the things that Mamma said, so Papa sat with them, night after night, and helped. Dall thought the same thing that Erinia thought: There were so many rules he'd never reach the end of them.

One evening Whymper showed Erinia and Nilaat a wonderful book with pictures of all the animals of the world. There were the whales and seals that Lena told stories about, the tiny deer that Papa said he had seen in New Arkhangel, the puffins with colored beaks that Old Man Kozevnikoff had told her about.

But most wonderful were the animals from Africa. Erinia was delighted to see that the giraffe got down on his knees to drink just as moose sometimes did. And she loved the patterns on the giraffe's fur. But the elephant and the hippopotamus and the rhinoceros had no fur at all, just folded, wrinkled naked skin. It was hard to believe that such animals were true.

When Nilaat went back to the winter houses, she told the Kaiyuh people about this book, and the next day they crowded into the store to see it. They were amazed at everything, but like Erinia, they were most amazed at the African animals. Only Simaaga pretended he had known about all those animals before.

The Indians came to the store every night after that to see all the other things the telegraph men had, the instruments and tools and maps and books. They were as interested in them as the people in the odinochka had been.

Erinia begged the telegraph men to show the people their uniforms. Fred Smith said he'd get his, and when he brought it back into the store from the barracks, the Kaiyuh women pulled the jacket out of his hands and turned it this way and that, exclaiming at how it was made. Fred looked so helpless when they took his shirt from him that Erinia had to laugh. They'd never seen buttons used with buttonholes, and neither had Erinia. All the Russian shirts and dresses were pulled over the head and tied at the neck. They'd never seen a shirt cut down the front, or the two shoulder pieces and back pieces called the yoke. They asked Fred to put the jacket on so they could see how it looked. When Fred put it on, he was dismayed to find that it didn't fit him anymore, but hung loosely.

"I've lost a lot of weight," he said sadly.

Simaaga was still aloof and refused to be impressed by anything the telegraph men had. Once he grew very angry and shouted when George Adams got ready to put some medicine in the eyes of a little Kaiyuh boy whose eyes were nearly sealed shut with a thick yellow discharge.

"What's *he* hollering about?" George asked Papa.

"Simaaga is the medicine man, and it's his job to cure sickness," said Papa. "He says *he* will cure the boy's eyes."

George put the medicine in anyway.

"If he can fix it, why hasn't he done so?" he asked.

Erinia knew that the telegraph men didn't like Simaaga, and they grumbled at the way the old man bullied people. George told Papa he was sorry that he'd given him his bowie knife. The men wanted to show Simaaga something that would amaze him so much that he'd stop pretending that he knew everything. But Simaaga couldn't be amazed, and so the telegraph men had to give up and admit he'd beaten them.

When the Kaiyuh men and boys played ball on the river, George and Fred and the other telegraph men joined the games and were as rowdy as anyone. They were like children, really, Erinia thought. Papa and Old Man

Kozevnikoff stood on the bank watching them. "After all," said Old Man Kozevnikoff, "they are really only boys, aren't they? It's not surprising that they will like to play." Erinia and Nilaat laughed to see one of the telegraph men playing hoops with the little children. You had to roll the hoop down the riverbank and try to spear it with a willow stick. The soldier wasn't very good at it, but he kept trying.

Whymper made a picture of the children playing the hoop game. Mamma told him that children could play this game only in the early spring because it was supposed to make the days longer, so Whymper wrote that at the bottom of the picture.

When the Kaiyuh people left for spring camp, they had all become good friends with the telegraph men, except for Simaaga, of course.

Chapter Seventeen

IN THE EVENINGS THE TELEGRAPH MEN AND PAPA AND OLD Man Kozevnikoff and Mikhail and Stepan spent hours telling stories to one another around the table, drinking tea and coffee and staying warm by the big stove.

Erinia and the boys and even Mamma and Lena came to listen every chance they got. Erinia thought nothing was so interesting as hearing about the lives the telegraph men had lived before they came north.

George Adams was from a place called San Francisco, which was built on hills, so that streets ran steeply up and down. In that city it never snowed.

George's father was an apothecary who made most of his money selling people flea powder to kill the fleas in their mattresses. George had been trained as an apothecary too, and that was how he had known what kind of medicine to put in the boy's eyes.

Fred Smith had been George's friend since they were boys. He and Fred had wanted to go fight in the war, but they couldn't because it would have cost too much to travel to the place where the war was going on. So they joined the telegraph men instead.

Whymper was from England, and he showed them that place on the map. It was so small Erinia felt a little sorry for Whymper, to have such a small country, when her Russia was so big and the Americans had a big country too. Dall was from almost as far away as England, a city called Boston, which was a much bigger place than San Francisco.

Whymper told Erinia about his little sister, who had a round thing she held over her head to keep the sun and the rain off her, and who could play music on the piano, which was something Erinia couldn't imagine. So Whymper drew her a picture of a little girl playing a piano, and then Erinia could see that a piano was like Dimitri's accordion laid flat, and with no buttons or pleats.

Everyone loved to watch Whymper work with his inks and his fast pen flying across the paper. He drew everything—

the odinochka and the costumes of the Indians; the big hunt, when the Indians trapped dozens of caribou inside the willow caribou fences. He made a big picture of the northern lights over the odinockha, but he wasn't happy with it.

"Trying to draw the northern lights is like trying to draw the wind," he said. And Erinia knew just what he meant, because the northern lights slid and shifted and slithered and were never still.

Sometimes he colored his pictures with little blocks of dried paint that he wet with water. Erinia had seen only red paint, but Whymper had ten different colors, each more beautiful than the last.

Whymper gave Erinia a new pencil to draw with and sharpened it with the little knife he kept in his pocket.

He told Erinia that the best way to really see something was to draw it. That way, you looked at the thing very carefully and noticed small details that you would never have noticed before. And it was true. When she drew, she saw things she'd never paid attention to before. Like the way things far away looked smaller, or the way shadows changed their shapes. She tried to draw the giraffes in the animal book, and the rhinoceros.

She didn't have much paper, just the backs of Old Man Kozevnikoff's store bills and letters, but Whymper showed her that birch bark was very good to draw on too. Erinia drew and drew every chance she got, but she never showed her drawings to anyone but Whymper because she wasn't entirely pleased with them.

When summer came, Dall spent all day collecting leaves and berries and bugs, things Erinia had hardly noticed before. He drew pictures of everything he collected, and sometimes he'd show Erinia a beautiful beetle or the hidden colors in the shining feather of a swallow.

Since the telegraph men came, Erinia had seen so many things that were all around her, things she might never have seen if they hadn't showed her.

Erinia was doing very well with her English speaking, so that summer Dall said he would teach her to read it as well.

Whenever he came back to Nulato from a field trip, he gave her reading lessons. He taught her the alphabet, and then he wrote out simple sentences for her and helped her figure out the words. Erinia thought English was very difficult because the sounds of the letters didn't stay the same, and so words were not pronounced the way they looked. And they weren't spelled the way they sounded. Not like Russian.

Papa had taught Erinia to read Russian when she was five, and so she taught Dall the Russian alphabet. He said it was harder than English, and Erinia said English was harder than Russian, so they couldn't agree on that.

∞

In early winter, after Erinia had been studying her English reading for many months, she began to read out loud at night after supper. Mamma would start the samovar and all the men would light their pipes, and sometimes they brought work to do, sewing or pegs to carve or harnesses to mend. She still read very slowly, but no one seemed to mind.

The book she was reading was called *Uncle Tom's Cabin*, which Fred Smith had loaned to her so she could practice her English. While she read, sometimes they all stopped work and held absolutely still, as if they didn't want to miss one word. She would pause every so often so they could all tell Mamma and Lena in Athabascan what she had read so far. The rest could all understand the English, though sometimes Papa or one of the telegraph men had to tell them what some words meant, or Erinia would have to ask one of the telegraph men to help her with the hard words she couldn't pronounce.

Erinia had to read over and over again the part where Eliza crosses the river on the ice floes. Of course they all realized that the river Eliza crossed wasn't anywhere near as wide as the Yukon, but still, they could just see how it would have been, and they sat listening each time with their faces tense.

And sometimes in a sad part of the story Erinia's throat

constricted, so that she could hardly speak, and she'd have to stop for a minute.

When she finished reading the last page of the last chapter, Mikhail looked at her sadly. "When a book ends," he said, "it's like someone has died."

Erinia felt the same way, and so she said maybe they should just start all over again right away. Everyone thought that was a good idea, and so she started the first chapter again the next night.

Uncle Tom's Cabin was about some black people who were owned as slaves in America. Erinia thought the Americans must be monsters to make people into slaves.

Papa said that his mother's people had owned slaves as well. They would capture people during a war, and those people would be their slaves. The people who owned them could even kill them if they wanted to.

"And," said Mikhail, "the Russians had serfs until just a few years ago. Not much better than slaves, serfs. My grandfather in Russia was a serf."

"How terrible people are to each other," Erinia said.

It was a very good thing to learn, Erinia thought. But when you began to learn, you learned such terrible things. It was better to be a little child and know nothing about the world.

Chapter Eighteen

LATER IN THE WINTER, WHEN THE NIGHTS GREW LONGER and longer, just before the bad cold came, it was time for the midwinter feast, the feast of mourning, which lasted a whole week.

The Kaiyuh people came from their scattered winter camps, and often the Kaltag people and people from upriver came as well.

Every year people who had had a death in their family would bring the ashes of their dead to the ceremony in a birch-bark basket or in a box carved of spruce. These containers were painted red. They would hang the box or the basket between four poles and put some of the things that had belonged to the dead person on another pole—their beads or tools or household objects.

Both Dall and Whymper had to be at Saint Michael at the time of the festival, and they were very upset to have to miss something so important to their research. Mamma told them about the ceremonies so Dall could write the customs down in his black book.

Mamma said the dead go upriver, and there they live just as they did when they were alive, except that the animals they hunt are different. Sometimes people find the bones of these animals, which the dead have not thrown in the river in the usual way, and they are huge, huge animals with long, curved tusks and grinding teeth as big as Erinia's foot.

Sometimes the dead come back to their old home, and people know that they're around when the dogs howl. They are waiting to be reborn in another body.

In the children's house are the souls of the children who are waiting to get into bodies. They can't wait to be born, so they fight with one another with charcoal axes to see who will be next. Mamma said that's why Indian babies are born with dark marks on the base of their spine, where the charcoal of the ax rubbed off.

When Mamma had finished telling Dall all about the festival, he had filled a whole notebook.

When the people came for the festival, the first thing the men did was set a tall spruce pole up in the middle of the odinochka yard. Then, at night, all the people dressed in their very best clothes and greased their hair and stuck swan down all over it. The men painted their faces with a soft black rock, and the women had theirs painted red.

Some of the Kaiyuh women had made jackets for their men that were like the army uniforms, except there were bright bands of beads and quills where the gold braid would be on the uniforms. These new-style jackets caused a lot of commotion. Everyone wanted to look at them and admire them, and the men who wore them were very proud.

In the bright moonlight the men stood in a line in their beautiful clothes while the women performed the mourning dance. They sang songs written especially about the ones who had died. These songs told what the person had done best, what they were noted for. One had been a good hunter, another a wonderful canoe maker. One woman who died had been a good sewer, and another a good storyteller.

Erinia thought it was very sad to hear good things about people when they weren't there anymore.

"What would people sing about if a person wasn't good at anything?" she whispered to Nilaat. She was worried about being that sort of person herself.

Nilaat gave Erinia a surprised look. "But Erinia," she whispered back, "everyone is good at *something*!"

Erinia wasn't sure that this was true, but she didn't argue.

The wife of a man who had died cut her hair in mourning for her husband, and while the other women were dancing, she cut her thighs with a knife and the blood ran into the beaten-down snow.

Erinia closed her eyes, but Nilaat said this was to show what a good husband he had been to the woman.

When the women finished, the men danced around the pole, singing "*Heeyo, heeyo.*" The women and children watched and sang too. They knew the men would sing "*Heeyo, heeyo*" around that pole for hours and hours and never get tired.

The crowd around the pole got bigger and bigger, and soon there were so many people in the yard of the odinochka that Nilaat and Erinia could hardly see a thing.

While they stood there, peering around people and under legs, two girls from downriver came up to them. "You look like boys," one said haughtily. "Like boys," said the other girl with contempt. They said that because Erinia and Nilaat didn't have blue lines tatooed on their chins like girls from downriver did. Nilaat and Erinia could think of nothing to say back to them, so they huffily turned their backs on the downriver girls and walked away.

There was feasting every night, and after all the people had eaten, food was put into the fire and burned for the dead so that they could get used to the new food they would have to eat when they went upriver.

The old men gave many speeches in the old language. And after the speeches the storytellers started. Their stories made all the children huddle together, they were so frightening. There were stories about the man of fire, who waited to burn up people walking in the woods, and about the water monsters and the woodsmen and giants and tiny dwarfs who used leaves for canoes. Erinia and Nilaat sat by the fire with the others, and Erinia was very glad that she didn't have far to go home.

In the daytime there were games, every game the people knew how to play.

Erinia and Nilaat thought the best game was the tying game, which both the young men and young women played. Two or three of them would tie up one of the players, and he would fight very hard to loosen himself. When he did, he would help the others catch someone else to tie up. It was very rough, but everyone loved to watch and play that game.

The high kick was fun too. A caribou-hide ball stuffed with fur was tied to a pole, and you had to jump high with both feet to kick the ball and then land back on your feet.

Even the telegraph men tried to do the high kick, but of course they weren't very good at it. When the men were finished with that contest and people had started to drift away, the little boys tried to kick the ball. Erinia wanted to try. She was sure she'd do it better than those boys did, but she was a girl and it was a game for boys only. And besides, she didn't want anyone to watch her, just in case she *wasn't* any good at it.

After a week of feasting and singing and dancing, and speeches and games and stories, everyone put away their good clothes and set out on the trail again, back to their winter camps.

Chapter Nineteen

AT THE DARKEST TIME OF YEAR, AFTER THE MOURNING festival, the sun peeked over the top of the hills just long enough to turn the sky beautiful pinks and purples, and then, almost right away, it went down again. They all hurried to do their outside work in the few hours of daylight and then went back inside by the fire, because it was the very coldest time of year as well, and no one traveled, unless it was necessary.

The telegraph men took the temperature with their instruments every day and recorded it in their official reports. Once it was nearly eighty below zero, they said. They said it had never been that cold, ever, where they came from. Dall taught Erinia how the thermometer worked, but she was never allowed to touch it. It was very fragile and they needed it for their scientific work, so they were very careful with it.

The telegraph men didn't like the cold, of course, but most of all they didn't like so much dark.

"In San Francisco," George said, "the days are always long, and it doesn't get dark until we've eaten our dinner."

The long darkness made the men think about their families and wonder what they were doing during Christmastime. The more they talked, the more homesick they became.

Papa said the Russian Christmas was a few weeks later than the American Christmas. In New Arkhangel at Christmastime there were always an extra lot of candles in the Russian church and some special songs that were sung only at that time.

Whymper said that in England some people brought a spruce tree into the house. Then they decorated it with candles and toys for the children, and candy.

"What is candy?" asked Erinia. The men looked at one another and laughed.

"Imagine a child who doesn't know what candy is!" said Sam.

They all looked at Erinia as if she'd suddenly become strange to them.

"I'll make some for you!" said Fred. "It's Christmas, and we must have some candy!"

When George looked a funny look at him, Fred said, "I'm a champion candymaker, for your information." George raised an eyebrow, but Fred told Erinia, "Go ask your mamma if I can borrow her big iron pot."

He sent one of the men to the barracks to get some of the expedition's sugar, and when Erinia came back with the pot, he mixed sugar and water together and set it to cook on the big stove in the store. Fred carefully stirred the mixture, watching the pot intently, putting his head every so often close to the pot.

"What are you doing that for?" asked Erinia.

"I'm listening to the sugar cooking. It will whisper a little when it is ready." Fred was very serious, his mouth folded up tightly.

"Whisper," said George, rolling his eyes at the other men. Erinia laughed. They were always making fun of each other, just like her brothers.

When the sugar did finally whisper to Fred, he dropped little bits of the syrup from a wooden spoon into a little dish of cold water, and when he was happy with the shape the drop made, he turned the mixture out of the big pot onto a wooden tray that he'd greased. The candy spread out all over the tray and smelled wonderful.

"Can we eat it now?" asked Erinia.

"No, it's not finished yet. As soon as it cools off, it must be pulled," said Fred. George and the other telegraph men looked at Fred's candy respectfully. "Well, I have to admit, it looks just like the candy my mother made," said George.

"It's *better* than the candy your mother made," answered Fred haughtily.

It seemed it would take forever for the candy to cool off, so Mamma made tea in the samovar, and while they were drinking it, the telegraph men told them what Christmas was like in their homes.

American children hung empty stockings by the fireplace on Christmas Eve. They believed that Saint Nicholas would come in the night and put something special in their stockings if they had been good children. If they had been bad, there would be just sticks in the stocking.

"I'll bet if you hang your stocking up, Erinia, Saint Nicholas will bring you something," said George. The telegraph men had knit stockings, which interested Mamma and Lena very much. One of the men had been teaching Lena how to knit. But no one in the odinochka had that kind of sock. They had a different kind of sock, made of rabbit skins turned outside in.

"I just have *tilth*," said Erinia. "Would that work?"

"Of course," cried Fred. "Saint Nicholas will be delighted to find something different waiting for him!"

When the candy in the tray was just warm, Fred called them all around and divided them into teams: Mamma and Papa, Lena and Old Man Kozevnikoff, George and Erinia, Pitka and Minook, Mikhail and Stepan, Whymper and Dall, and the other two telegraph men. Fred said he'd supervise and make sure they were doing the pulling properly. Then he passed around the tin of lard and told them they must grease their hands or the candy would stick dreadfully.

He gave each team a ball of warm candy. He showed them how they must stand opposite each other and pull the candy back and forth until it turned almost white and you couldn't see through it anymore.

It *was* very sticky. Mamma sent such a sharp look to her that Erinia knew Mamma was thinking about the time Erinia had gotten pitch in her hair when she was little.

They pulled the candy back and forth, back and forth, catching up the long threads that dropped down, until it was white and streaky looking. Lena shrieked because Old Man Kozevnikoff was pulling too fast, and Pitka and Minook made a dreadful mess and had to ball it all back up again and start over. When they were finished, Fred took all their long, pulled pieces and put them back on the greased tray. He cut the long pieces into short pieces and then it was ready to eat.

And that was candy. This kind of candy was called taffy, and the telegraph men said there were many, many other kinds of candy as well. Never had Erinia tasted anything more delicious. She was not the only one. They all liked it, even Mamma.

Then George showed Erinia how to hang her rabbit sock up by the window.

"Did *you* ever get sticks?" she asked George.

"Never!" said George.

"Ha," said Fred, but George sent him a look, so he didn't say anything else.

And in the morning there *was* something in Erinia's stocking: five shining brass army buttons with insignias on them, a new pencil, and a package of little brown things called raisins. Erinia knew, of course, that the telegraph men had put those things in there. She didn't believe that there was a Saint Nicholas. But still, it *seemed* like magic.

And there were packages tied up in white cloth for everyone in the odinochka. There was a pen for Papa and a little pair of scissors for Mamma, a magnet for Pitka and a magnifying glass for Minook, an American pipe for Old Man Kozevnikoff and safety pins for Lena. Stepan's package had suspenders, and Mikhail got a pair of wool army socks.

"Now I can hang my stocking next Christmas," Mikhail told Erinia.

Everyone gathered around the table in the store and drank cups and cups of tea and ate bread and some of the soldiers' delicious bacon, and Old Man Kozevnikoff made blinis, which he always made on any special occasion.

After breakfast the soldiers sang Christmas songs. One had such funny words they had to laugh—*falalalala-lalalala*—and Erinia wanted them to sing it over and over.

"In Boston we have a turkey for our Christmas dinner," said Dall. That was a big bird, bigger than any they had in Russian America, Papa explained. "We have ham," Sam said. Whymper said when he was a boy, they always had a goose.

"In the winter?" asked Mamma when Papa had translated.

"Well, our geese don't go south in the winter," said Whymper. "Well, I mean, the wild ones do, but not the other ones." When Mamma looked puzzled, he said, "Geese and chickens and birds like that are raised for people to eat. You can go to the butcher and buy one at any time of year." Mamma looked amazed when Papa told her what he'd said. Erinia was amazed as well. Imagine not having to hunt for your meat.

Mamma and Erinia had caught some fat ptarmigan in their snares, and so they had those for their Christmas dinner. The telegraph men made some of the dried potatoes into a mush and made some applesauce. And there were canned peaches, too. Mamma knew this was a special dinner for the soldiers, so she brought out her precious seal oil, which had come all the way from the ocean, and showed them how to dip pieces of ptarmigan into it. It made everything taste better, Mamma said. But the telegraph men didn't seem to like it very much.

"And what do you do at night, after Christmas dinner?" asked Erinia. Fred said that children would play with their new toys and that people would come around from house to house and sing.

"We always had a dance at night," said Sam.

George decided they must teach everyone an American dance called the waltz. Papa said he didn't think the waltz was an American dance, because the people in New Arkhangel had danced the waltz. "In fact," he said, "the creole girls there were so useless that they couldn't sew or cook, but they all knew how to waltz!"

"Yes," said Whymper. "And we waltz in England as well."

"Maybe it's not an American dance," said George. "But it's very popular, and we're going to dance it!"

None of the telegraph men had an instrument, so they took turns singing while all the others danced. They sang "Beautiful Dreamer," "Flow Gently, Sweet Afton," "Green Grow the Lilacs," and the one Erinia liked best, "Sweet Evelina."

They had to step forward and right, and back and

forward again, to trace a sort of box with their feet, and count in time to the music, one-two-three, one-two-three.

The men who weren't singing—Pitka and Minook, Stepan and Papa, Old Man Kozevnikoff and even Mikhail, with his lame foot—waltzed with Erinia and Mamma and Lena and with one another. One-two-three, one-two-three. Everyone had to concentrate very hard, looking at their feet at first, but when they got used to it, it was wonderful. A sweeping, swooping dance, not a jiggling-up-and-down dance, not a boot-stomping dance, but a quite different dance. It was thrilling to swoop down the long room and back up again, dipping and gliding like swallows.

They danced for a long time, until everyone was tired and the ones who were singing were hoarse, and when it was time to go to bed, Erinia was sorry because she thought it was the most delightful day she'd ever spent.

Chapter Twenty

W HEN THE TELEGRAPH MEN HAD BEEN WORKING FOR two years, they'd finished the surveying and were digging the holes for the telegraph poles. This was very hard work. In the coldest part of winter the ground was so hard they had to use a pick to dig, and they could dig only six holes a day. Their shovels were useless in the winter.

But soon they would be able to string the copper wires, and then it would be all finished. Papa and Old Man Kozevnikoff could hardly wait for the day a telegraph message would come to the odinochka.

One winter morning Lena was showing Erinia how the Aleuts braided grass to make grass mats.

"This grass is not as good as our Aleutian grass," Lena complained, "but it's good enough so you can see how the braiding is done."

Then the dogs began to bark their visitor warning. As soon as Lena heard the dogs, her cheeks turned pink and she jumped up from the table. "Maybe Elia's coming," she said. He hadn't been home for a long time. Of course, he was married now, so of course, Lena said, he was busy, and of course she was glad that he'd found a good, hardworking girl. But still, it was hard to have him gone for so long.

Lena and Erinia rushed from the Kozevnikoffs' kitchen, and Old Man Kozevnikoff and Papa and Mamma hurried out of the store and went to the bank to look down the river. The telegraph men had gone with Minook and Pitka to hunt for caribou across the river, but Mikhail and Stepan came running from the woodpile to watch the river too.

They all shaded their eyes against the bright winter sun, and at last they saw him. One team, with only one driver. Not Elia. Not tall enough.

Erinia was sorry to see Lena's round face lose its happy look.

They asked one another who it could be and waited impatiently until the team came up the bank.

Lena and Mamma went inside to get the tea ready in the samovar. Mamma told Erinia crossly to put on her parka if she was going to stand outside. Unexpected visitors made Mamma nervous because they seldom brought good news.

It was Lukin, and everyone could see from his face that something was wrong.

"Welcome," said Papa, but his face had grown as somber as Lukin's.

Lukin just nodded. He bent to untie the lashings on the sled and pulled out a small mail packet from his pack. Stepan and Mikhail started to see to the dogs, but Lukin stopped them.

"You'd better hear this news too," he said. "You can take care of the dogs in a minute."

Stepan and Mikhail looked at each other.

They all filed into the store, and after he'd pulled off his parka and greeted Mamma and Lena, Lukin threw the mail packet on the counter.

"What's this about?" asked Old Man Kozevnikoff.

"The purchase went through," said Lukin quietly.

Papa and Old Man Kozevnikoff looked so shocked that Erinia was frightened.

"What does he mean, Papa?"

Papa pulled her to his side and stroked her hair. At last he said, "Russia has sold Russian America to the United States." Lena covered her mouth with her hand, and Mamma looked grim. "There was a rumor last year." Papa shook his head sadly. "We thought it was just a rumor."

She peered into his face. "I don't understand, Papa."

"We don't understand either, Erinia."

Old Man Kozevnikoff opened all the dispatches that the company had sent from New Arkhangel. The purchase had taken place in the spring of 1867, but it had taken some time for the news to come from Russia to New Arkhangel. Then there had been a long wait for a ship going from New Arkhangel to the Aleutians, and from the Aleutians the news had had to be carried over the trail to the Kuskokwim River and then by dog team to Saint Michael. That was thousands of versts, so the dispatches had taken many months to get to them.

The men stayed up all night by the samovar talking about the news.

In the morning, when Erinia and Mamma came to bring them their breakfast, they were still talking.

Mamma set down the wooden platter of fish with a thump and then turned to Papa.

"What will happen to us?" she asked sharply.

Papa ran his palm over his mustache.

"Don't worry, Malanka. It's not so bad," he said. But Erinia thought he didn't really mean it, because nothing good ever happened when Papa smoothed his mustache like that.

"An American company has bought everything from the Russian American Company. The Alaska Commercial Company," Papa said. "We can keep working for the new company. All the people can stay to work for the Americans at the same pay."

The Nulato odinochka would still be a trading post, but of course the instructions would come in English now.

Russian Americans who were born in Russia, and Russian Americans who were creoles, had three years to decide if they wanted to stay when the Americans took over. If they didn't want to stay, the Russian government would pay their way to Russia.

Mamma looked wild-eyed when Papa told her that. "No," she said.

"Of course not," said Papa.

He and Old Man Kozevnikoff were creoles, just like Lukin and Mikhail and Stepan and all the people on the Yukon who worked for the company. They'd never been to Russia.

So they would stay and be ruled by the Americans.

Lukin went back to Saint Michael after breakfast. That afternoon the boys and the telegraph men came back from hunting with two caribou in the sleds. The telegraph men whooped and pounded one another on the back when Old Man Kozevnikoff told them about the purchase. Pitka and Minook dropped their packs and sank down on the benches around the table. They were too surprised to say anything.

One of the telegraph men ran to the barracks and came back with the American flag they'd had on the wall. They rushed outside to hang it on a fence pole, and when they had finished that, they shot off their rifles to celebrate.

Erinia put her hands over her ears, and Mamma and Lena ran to the kitchen to get away from the noise of the guns. Erinia felt very cross with the telegraph men for acting like children when the rest of them were all so sad.

At last the telegraph men noticed that no one from the odinochka was celebrating with them.

They came into the store and looked at the men sitting around the samovar.

Dall was very disappointed that Papa and Old Man Kozevnikoff were not pleased and excited about being Americans.

"America is the greatest country in the world," he said.

"Yes?" said Papa. He looked very tired.

"Yes," said George very earnestly. "We have democracy and progress. Voting. We vote for our leaders. That's democracy."

Papa gave George a long look before he said, "The slaves didn't vote."

There was quiet in the room, and then Dall sat down

on the bench next to Minook and didn't say any more.

"The slaves are free now," said George. "That's what the war was about. President Lincoln freed the slaves."

"Lincoln was a good man," said Papa. "But he is dead."

"But surely," said George, "it will be better to be governed by the Americans than by the Russians?"

"There's an old Russian saying," said Papa. "Better the devil you know than the one you don't know." Old Man Kozevnikoff looked at Papa and smiled a little.

Erinia thought the telegraph men all looked bewildered. George sat down now and looked at Papa.

"You've heard about the cruelty of the early Russian hunters, I'm sure." Papa pointed to Old Man Kozevnikoff with his pipe. "Kozevnikoff will tell you what his grandfather had to say about that time," he said.

"Oh, yes," said Old Man Kozevnikoff. "Terrible stories. Terrible."

"But that was a long time ago," said Papa. "When she heard of the behavior of those hunters, Empress Catherine herself ordered that the cruelty stop and that the Aleuts be treated with respect. Our new brothers, she called them. And Yuri tells us that in America the American soldiers now are killing many Indian people and moving them from their land. They are not calling those Indian people 'our new brothers.' I think that America is not so good to its native people as Russia is."

The telegraph men looked uncomfortable, but they didn't say anthing, so Papa went on.

"Sometimes things were not so good, working for the company, but the Russians did many things for us. Kozevnikoff and Lukin, me, Mikhail and Stepan—we were all raised by the Russians. They gave us a good education. Of course we know that the company took care of us for their own benefit as well as ours. They needed trained workers. And we had to agree to be employed by the company for a while, five years, ten years, to pay back our education. But they built hospitals and orphanages and schools, not just for the children with Russian fathers, but for the other children as well.

"And those who've grown too sick or old to work, they get a pension. Kozevnikoff was looking forward to that pension. Now he will not get it."

Erinia could see that the telegraph men had never thought of such things and didn't know how to answer.

Papa pulled his pipe out of his pocket and filled it with tobacco.

"And now we are Americans," he said. He lit his pipe with a match, which just showed Erinia how upset he was. On an ordinary day he would never waste a precious match on a pipe.

"What will happen to us all? Will there be work for everyone? Will the schools carry on? What about the

Russian missions? Will America let us creoles be citizens?" Papa leaned forward and pointed to the telegraph men with the stem of his pipe. "Will America let *us* vote?"

Dall moved his shoulder a little to show that he didn't know. George said stoutly that he was sure that the American government would be just as good to the people as the Russians were, but he didn't sound so sure anymore.

When Erinia went outside, she saw the American flag hanging limply by the fence. They were Americans. Not Russians. Americans.

Erinia felt exactly as she did when she had done something bad and been criticized. Except that this time she didn't know what she had done to be bad.

How could Russia have given them away? Why did she abandon them? All those miles of lovely tundra and river and tall spruce trees. Why didn't Russia want them anymore?

For the first time Erinia felt what it was like to be Mamma and have everything change so suddenly.

Papa followed Erinia outside and held her hand while they both looked at the flag.

Erinia whispered, because she felt ashamed. "Papa, why didn't Russia want us? Why did she sell us to the Americans?"

Papa looked down at her.

"Well, Erinia, these are very complicated matters. I'm not sure I understand why myself. I think it's like when a family has too many children and they let someone else have the baby. Maybe Russia had too many people, too many children, too many children scattered too far away. Or maybe the company wasn't making enough money."

"But I like to be a Russian, Papa! I like to speak Russian and look at Russia on the big map and say the names. And Papa! The kazachka!"

Papa smiled. "But Erinia, you don't have to give up speaking Russian, or any of the other things! We're Americans now, but we can be Russians, too, and Athabascans and Tlingits. And Aleuts. It's like when you will be married and have children. You'll belong to your new family, but you'll still belong to your old family. Being an American is just a new thing. It doesn't take anything away."

"But Papa, you said the Americans are not good to the Indians."

"Well, maybe I shouldn't have spoken of such things in front of you, Erinia. After all, we don't really know what will happen. Our telegraph men are Americans and they are good men. So maybe Americans are better than we've heard."

"We had so much fun before, Papa."

"Well, did you think that all the fun was going to be

gone? Dimitri and Lev are not gone, are they? Or Yuri? They can still play music for us, whether they're Russian subjects or not. Wherever people are, there'll be dancing and singing. Don't you worry about that. All the fun isn't gone. In fact, you'll probably not even see anything different for a long, long time."

And then Erinia felt better.

Papa picked her up and rocked her back and forth for a long while. He was so kind and gentle, her papa.

Chapter Twenty-one

B UT PAPA WAS WRONG. THE CHANGES DIDN'T COME SLOWLY, as he'd said. Some changes came fast.

For one thing, there were so many new things to learn.

It wasn't long before the Alaska Commercial Company asked for an inventory of the goods in the store. That meant that Papa and Old Man Kozevnikoff had to count everything and measure and weigh it.

Erinia helped them by bringing lists of things she'd counted in the storerooms, written half in English and half in Russian. She counted beads and bells and hats, and she even found a box of tin spoons that had been put so far back on the top shelf that no one knew it was there.

But she couldn't help them with the weights and measurements.

These had to be done in American measurements, not Russian. They had no American scales or measuring instruments, so after they'd measured with the Russian scales and measuring rods, they had to convert.

The telegraph men had all gone to Saint Michael to get their supplies for the spring, but they'd left behind their conversion chart. The chart showed how to change Russian measurements to American measurements. Without the chart Papa and Old Man Kozevnikoff couldn't have done the report at all. But the chart was written in tiny print, and Papa had to hold it very close to his eyes to read it.

If a beaver pelt measured 10 verchoks, they had to multiply 10 times 1.75 to find out how long the pelt was in inches. An arshin was 28 American inches and a sazhen was 7 feet, and a vedro was 2.70 gallons, and 10 charkas made 2.16 pints. A pud was 36.11 pounds, and a verst was .66 of a mile. A chetvert was 49 pounds.

Money was less difficult. A Russian ruble was about half of an American dollar, and a kopek was about half of an American cent, so that was easy to figure out.

Their paperwork took them a long time. Old Man Kozevnikoff couldn't read, so Papa peered at the chart and read it out while Old Man Kozevnikoff did the figuring, thrusting his fingers into his hair when the problem was difficult. Between them they managed to get the inventory done, but when they were finished, Papa's eyes had a pinched look and Old Man Kozevnikoff's white hair was standing on end.

And then, just before the ice broke up, Kate came home from Ikogmute. She'd gotten a ride on one of the sleds that were freighting food for the telegraph men.

Kate didn't look like she belonged to them anymore, really. She'd grown tall and she wore her braids wrapped around her head the way the ladies did in the photographs the telegraph men had.

Erinia felt almost shy with her sister, as if she were a stranger. And she could tell that Minook and Pitka felt the same way, because they didn't tease her the way they would have before she left home.

Kate wouldn't be going back to school because the Russian priest had decided to go back to Russia and the school was closed down. Kate was very sorry that the school was closed, but Erinia was glad. Now she needn't worry that Papa would take it in his head to send her to Ikogmute when she was old enough.

Erinia thought Kate was a lot more interesting than she used to be. She didn't keep her head down in the old Indian way anymore. She was still quiet. But she had opinions. She'd never had opinions before.

At school she'd learned to make all the Russian Easter cakes and pastries that Papa had loved so much in New Arkhangel, and she had read a lot of the Russian books Papa had read when he was in school. Papa was very proud of her.

But Mamma was not pleased about the new Kate. The new Kate had become very fussy about keeping clean. It wasn't so much what she said, but the way she held her hands, arched at the wrists, fingers and thumbs together. And the way she held her skirts off the ground.

"Erinia, you're getting to be a big girl," Kate said. "You must comb and braid your hair every morning. And you must wash it more often. Look at this!" Kate tried to pull a comb through some snarls that had been growing at the top of Erinia's braids. Kate made so much trouble about Erinia's hair that Erinia wished she could cut it off again the way it was when she was younger.

The Alaska Commercial Company wanted its men to travel farther and trade harder than the Russian company had. In the spring Lukin came up the Yukon in his big boat on his way to Nuklakayet for the trading festival there. There was still some ice from breakup on the river, but Lukin said that dodging ice made the trip more interesting.

The trading festival took place way upriver where the Tanana River joined the Yukon. In that place a lot of

Indians met from all over to dance and trade and hold games. They came from way up the river at Fort Yukon and from all the way up and down the Tanana River. The new American company wanted Lukin to buy all the furs that were offered there and make sure no one else got them.

Minook was going to travel with Lukin, and he was very excited about that. He'd never been so far upriver before.

Erinia wished she could go too.

When he arrived, Lukin gave Papa a letter he'd brought with him, and Papa was delighted.

"From Petr at New Arkhangel," he said. Petr had been Papa's friend when he was a boy, and he was the only one in New Arkhangel who still wrote to Papa. This letter had been traveling to Papa for many months, and the oil-cloth packet that it was wrapped in was very stained and battered looking. Erinia wanted to hear what was in the letter right away, but Papa said he would read it to them later when they were all together.

After supper, when they were drinking tea, Papa at last took the letter out of its wrappings and smoothed the pages carefully on the table. "Now we will know what has been going on since we became Americans," he said.

Erinia was sleepy, so she stretched her arms out on the table and laid her head on them while Papa read. She watched the smoke curl from Old Man Kozevnikoff's pipe up to the ceiling and imagined the red carpets and pretty creole girls waltzing in New Arkhangel.

> My dear Ivan,
> Greetings to you and your family from your old friend Petr. I pray that this letter finds you in the best of health.
>   Probably you haven't heard that New Arkhangel is now called Sitka. And Russian America is renamed Alaska. I wish those were the only changes—

"Alaska?" interrupted Minook. "Why did they name it that?"

Papa shook his head. "I don't know."

"There's a place in the Aleutians called Alyeska," said Old Man Kozevnikoff. "Maybe it's named for that."

"Perhaps," Papa said, and began to read again.

> I wonder how the purchase has affected your life. Perhaps this letter will not reach you at the odinochka. Perhaps you have gone someplace else. Here our lives have become a misery.

Papa paused to give a startled look to Old Man Kozevnikoff, who looked anxiously back, and Erinia sat up straight, wide-awake now.

The governor did everything he could to make the changeover gracious.

He was leaving behind all his furniture and goods so that the American general who was taking his place would be comfortable. But as soon as the new flag was flying on the flagpole in front of the governor's quarters, the new American commander, General Davis, turned to the governor and ordered him and his wife to move out immediately. He did not even give them time to find another place. Everyone was shocked at the bad behavior of General Davis. He has continued to be a tyrant in every respect.

The American soldiers stationed here are barbarians.

They make alcohol in every barracks, and there is drunkenness and violence everywhere. No one is safe.

All our orphanages and hospitals have been closed, and the Americans have no plans to open them again. The Americans don't provide any schools for the children, either. Russia sent money to keep the schools open because they want the creole children educated, even if they aren't Russian anymore. You know Vasilii went to Saint Petersburg, but now I don't know what will happen to him.

Papa looked up from the letter. "Petr's son was sent to Russia to become a doctor," he explained. "He was to be the first creole doctor.

Perhaps he will be allowed to finish his training, but perhaps not, since the Russian American Company had been paying for it and the company no longer exists. I've heard nothing from Vasilii and I'm very worried.

The Americans don't call us creoles. They call us half-breeds and it is said with a sneer, though most of us are better educated and have better skills than the American soldiers, who seem to be almost illiterate. They have no respect for what the creoles have done over the last hundred years. Perhaps things will change for the better, but like everyone else in New Arkhangel, I am discouraged and weary. I send my best regards and wishes for your health and safety.

Your old friend,

Petr

Papa put the letter down.

Old Man Kozevnikoff's eyes had narrowed and his jaw was clenched. He punched his fist into his other palm. "By god, I wish I was there. I'd teach them respect," he said.

"It's the same in Saint Michael," said Lukin. "The soldiers at the new fort are arrogant and out of control. Lots of liquor. The same at Fort Yukon and Fort Gibbons. People in the camps around the fort and the store are drinking a lot, I hear."

Mamma looked anxiously at Minook. Fort Gibbons was near Nuklakayet. She wouldn't want him to go to Nuklakayet with Lukin if that was the way things were.

Papa and Old Man Kozevnikoff liked their rum ration when it came, but that rum was for just one night, to have a good time and dance and sing. If people could have liquor any time they wanted, every day, they might not do any work. And worst of all, they might become violent and dangerous. Old Man Kozevnikoff had seen it happen.

It was as Papa and Lukin and Old Man Kozevnikoff thought it would be. Things were worse with the Americans. No hospitals, no schools, no order. And troubles with alcohol.

Papa and Old Man Kozevnikoff were very quiet for many days after Petr's letter came. Belonging to America had brought many changes, and so far none of them were good.

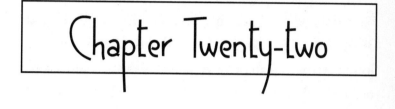

Chapter Twenty-two

AFTER LUKIN AND MINOOK HAD GONE ON THEIR WAY TO Nuklakayet, the telegraph men came back from Saint Michael with their supplies and got ready for a long trip of their own. Dall and Whymper and some of the telegraph men were going all the way up the river to Fort Yukon to explore and make maps for the telegraph line. Now that the country belonged to America, there might be some changes in the route the telegraph line would take.

Erinia and Mamma helped them make hardtack and dry meat for their grub box, but Erinia felt sad.

Fort Yukon was a long way, almost 900 versts, 575 miles in the American way, and so the men would be gone most of the summer. She'd miss Dall and Whymper, who always taught her so much.

Before he left, Lukin had said that there had been a lot of sickness that year on the Kuskokwim River and the lower Yukon and all the way along the coast. Many people had died. When he said that, Mamma tied dried fish tails over all the doors. That was an Indian charm to keep sickness away. Kate said that the fish tails smelled bad, but Mamma gave her a hard look and Kate didn't say any more.

When the families came from the Kaiyuh to fish, all of the people at the odinochka were sad to see how small the group had become. In every family someone had died, and in some families it was more than one.

Old Kkaabaa had been sick all winter, coughing and hot with fever, and not long after the families had settled into the fish camp, she died as well.

After everything that was customary had been done to mourn Kkaabaa properly, Nilaat brought her little bundle of things and came to live at last at the odinochka.

Mamma fixed up a little room for her right next to the fur room. She said that Erinia and Nilaat couldn't sleep in the same room because they would never get any sleep, the way the two of them carried on, but that was all right.

Lena got all of the clothes Erinia had outgrown from the storage-room shelves and mended them, and Mamma made Nilaat a new apron from the white cloth the telegraph men had left behind. When they had finished sewing her new clothes, Nilaat put her caribou-skin dress and her boot-pants and her rabbit underwear away on the shelves. Then she put on the Russian underwear and the blue calico dress Erinia had worn when she was younger, and the apron. They all stared at her, she looked so different. Nilaat looked down at the dress and smoothed it with her rough little fingers. And then she smiled her most brilliant smile. "I look beautiful, don't I?" she said. The calico dress was longer than her Indian dress and much fuller, so she kept getting her legs tangled in it when she ran.

"Just pull it up high when you run, over your knees. That's what I do," said Erinia.

When the fall came, Nilaat would not leave with the Kaiyuh people. She would never leave again. And she wouldn't have to work so hard and be treated so harshly ever again. Erinia thought she would never wish for anything else now that Nilaat was with them, safe and happy.

Within a very short time Nilaat's cheeks filled out and her bony little wrists and arms were rounder and sturdier looking. Old Man Kozevnikoff would pinch her cheeks and smile.

"Our little Nilaat! Look at you! Like a plump rabbit! Like a ptarmigan! Soon you'll be as fat as my Lena!" To his way of thinking, and Lena's, too, it was almost an offense to be too thin.

∞

When the king salmon run was over and the dog salmon run was almost finished, Major Kennicott unexpectedly came from his headquarters at Saint Michael. The first year the telegraph men came he had often been in Nulato, but he hadn't been there for a long time. Erinia was glad to see him again, but he was much more serious than he had been. He said he had something important to tell his men, so he would wait for them to come back from Fort Yukon. He was very impatient. He'd go to the riverbank every day and walk up and down, looking upriver.

"What could be keeping them?" he'd say.

At last, on a gray day, their boats came. Erinia scampered up and down the bank carrying this bag and that for them, asking Dall every question she could think of.

Whymper had brought Erinia sketches of the little ground squirrels that lived at Fort Yukon. They stood on their hind legs and rubbed their hands together like little worried people. How Erinia wished she could see a ground squirrel.

The telegraph men told her things as she went in and out and as they unpacked. The Indians way upriver spoke differently from the Indians at Nulato, and their ways were a little different as well. Whymper showed Erinia a drawing he'd made of the fancy way those Indians painted their faces for a celebration, and a drawing of a baby in a birch-bark carrier. The baby had a beautiful little beaded suit on with a hood, and a bone through his nose.

Whymper said he'd show the rest of his pictures to Erinia after supper. But right now there was no time because the major had called a meeting of everyone around the samovar. Mamma was making the tea, and Papa and the major and Old Man Kozevnikoff and Lena were waiting for them in the store.

The sky had grown darker, and as they sat down to the steaming samovar big raindrops began to fall. The smell of wet dust came through the open door and the room grew suddenly cold.

Papa got up to shut the door.

The major stood up. He had to speak loudly to be heard over the drumming of the rain.

"I waited so I could tell you all at once," he said. "While you were in Fort Yukon, I received some news at Saint Michael that will, I think, surprise you all." He cleared his throat. "We've had good times in this room with our friends."

He lifted his cup of tea to Papa and Old Man Kozevnikoff. Then he laid his hand on Erinia's head.

"And what would we have done without our Erinia to keep us cheerful?"

Then Erinia knew what the major would say next, and

her throat began to ache the way it did when you knew you'd lost something.

"We're going home, boys," the major said.

All the faces around the table went still, as if no one knew if that was good news or bad.

"The Western Union Telegraph Expedition is no more," said the major.

There would be no telegraph line. While they'd been working so hard to build it, on the other side of the world people had put a cable under the Atlantic Ocean, which made their telegraph line unnecessary. So all the work they had done had been for nothing.

The telegraph men looked at one another with unbelieving faces. All those hard times with no food. All the horrible days with frozen faces and fingers, all the long, hard trails on snowshoes, all the days holed up in a canvas tent in bitter cold weather. Fighting those swarms of mosquitoes. And worst of all, all those hundreds and hundreds of postholes, dug out of the frozen ground with dull, unsharpened picks.

"All that work for nothing," said Fred.

"For nothing," said George.

They were to go to Saint Michael as fast as they could to catch the last boat out to San Francisco in California.

Of course someone had to be sent immediately to the telegraph crews who were still working in the hills. The others had to start to get their gear together for the trip downriver to Saint Michael.

The telegraph men had found their tongues and they began to talk all at once, stepping on one another's words as they hurried to the barracks to start their packing.

Dall looked frantic. He had so many boxes of animal skeletons and specimens for the museum that he was sure he'd never be packed up in time to go when the boats left.

Erinia and the others sat in the store by the samovar without speaking, while the rain beat down on the hard-packed dirt outside the door.

They'd all miss the telegraph men. All those young, lively voices, the joking and games they'd had. Mamma wouldn't ever again have anyone as interested in the ways of her people as Whymper and Dall had been. Erinia wouldn't walk in the woods with Dall anymore to hear something new about the creatures there. She wouldn't watch Whymper drawing, his face distorted with concentration. The telegraph men had made all their lives exciting, and Erinia thought with dread of the drabness they'd leave behind.

With the telegraph men it was as if they'd climbed to a high place where they could see beyond the odinochka to the whole world. And when the telegraph came, they thought they would talk to that world and be part of it.

They all had felt that they were helping with something big and important. Now they would be part of nothing.

There would be only ten at the odinochka again. Ten sounded just too lonesome, and it seemed they were suddenly so far away from everything again.

Erinia wanted to cry, but she was too old to behave like a baby.

PART THREE

The Relatives

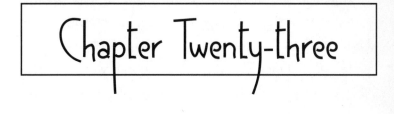

Chapter Twenty-three

THE WINTER AFTER THE TELEGRAPH MEN LEFT SEEMED LONG and dreary. Erinia often lay awake in her bed in the morning, not even wanting to get up and start the day. The telegraph men had left behind a dozen thick green wool army blankets. Erinia had two of them on her bed, and so every morning she was reminded again of all the good times they'd had when the telegraph men were with them. With her forefinger she traced the insignia woven into the blanket, as if that were a magic spell she could work to bring them back.

"Oh, I wish, I wish they were still here," she said out loud. Without the telegraph men there were no surprises. Nothing to look forward to. She felt very sorry for herself.

It wasn't just the telegraph men she missed.

Papa had said there would still be singing and dancing even if they weren't Russian anymore, but he was wrong about that.

Lev and Dimitri and Nikolai didn't work for the Alaska Commercial Company anymore, so when the trade goods were delivered, there was no accordion, no balalaika, no Cossack dance. Last fall there was no Yuri to fiddle for them, for he'd gone back to California, where the sun never stopped shining. They all had gone to work in other places. More exciting places, thought Erinia.

There was not even dancing at the festival for the dead because there was no festival. There had been so much sickness and death everywhere that those left hadn't the energy to gather the food and do the sewing necessary for the festival. Many fewer Kaiyuh people came to trade, and instead of the strong, firm line that came across the ice, they came in little groups that seemed to straggle wearily. Simaaga had died in the influenza epidemic, and so the last time the Kaiyuh people did come, they didn't do the greeting dance. And the rowdy games on the ice and the old riddles around the fire didn't happen. It was as if the whole world had grown very tired and dispirited.

"But at least you are with us," Erinia often told Nilaat. "Without you and Kate this winter would have been too gloomy to bear."

"The girls," Old Man Kozevnikoff called Erinia and Kate and Nilaat. "Where are my girls!" he would bellow when it was time for tea.

But Erinia knew Old Man Kozevnikoff missed the way things had been. "He is sadder than I am," Erinia said to Nilaat. "He liked it so much when the odinochka was full of people and everyone was laughing and having a good time."

It was a cold, cold winter. It was so cold that it was hard to keep the rooms in the odinochka warm enough, and the windows were all frosted so heavily that it was dark inside the rooms even when it was daylight. Old Man Kozevnikoff would thump the frost off the sealskin windows in the store, and some light would come in for a while, but then the frost would form again and no sunshine could get through. And the frost on Mamma's mica windows was so thick it couldn't be scraped off.

If the telegraph men had been there, they would have read the numbers on the thermometer to see how cold it was, but without those instruments they had to use the old ways to tell—by the frost on the trees and the sound of the snow underfoot and the way the chimney smoke rose.

They all wore their heavy moccasins inside as well as outdoors because the floor was so cold. If Mamma dropped water on the floor, it froze right away and made a treacherous slippery place.

Erinia thought they'd all be happier if she had another book to make the nights pass quickly. They had tired long ago of hearing *Uncle Tom's Cabin*, and even Mikhail and Stepan didn't want to hear it again. Sometimes they persuaded Lena to tell the Aleut stories she had told them when Pitka and Kate and Erinia were children. And sometimes even Mamma would tell one of the long Athabascan stories about people who turned into animals.

Kate had read all the Russian books the priest at Ikogmute had brought from Russia, and so she told them the stories of those books while they sat around the table and drank tea.

Papa had also read those books in the classroom at New Arkhangel, so together he and Kate would try to remember just how each story went. It was good to have those stories, but they were naked stories, without all the little things that made the stories in a book so wonderful, without all the descriptions that made you see just what it was like in the story. And besides, Erinia thought the girls in the stories were very silly, like Tatyana in *Eugene Onegin*, who carried on so about nothing.

Pitka had been especially lonesome all winter because Minook had stayed at Nuklakayet to work for the trader up there.

In the early summer Papa and Old Man Kozevnikoff

and Lukin went to the trading festival at Nuklakayet. Pitka looked up the river every day, waiting for their return. But when they all came back, Minook wasn't with them. Pitka looked sadly at Papa and then stooped to pick up the bundles from the boat.

"Where's Minook?" asked Mamma sharply. Papa bent down to tie the boat to the stake driven into the bank. Then he looked a funny look at Mamma.

"Minook has found a wife."

Mamma's face went stiff.

"Her Indian name is Yawhodelno, but Minook calls her Liza, her baptism name."

Mamma still didn't change her expression, so Papa went on. "Her father is a very important man, and Minook had to give a lot of presents to win him over." Erinia knew he hoped that would impress Mamma.

It was the custom for the new husband to stay with the girl's family and work for them for several years before the young couple made their own home, so Papa said he hoped Minook would be able to get along with that old man.

"He's pretty tough," Papa said. He gave Pitka a look and Pitka smiled. If Papa said that, he must be really ornery.

Mamma wanted to know the important things. Could Liza sew? Was she a hard worker? Papa wasn't much help with these questions.

"She's very pretty," he said, but Mamma just made a sound of disgust. Erinia knew that meant, what good was pretty if she couldn't work?

While she was helping unload the boats, Erinia thought about how contrary she was. She wanted new things to happen, and then when they did happen, like Minook getting married, she was upset because things had changed. She felt very cross, so she complained. "I should see this Liza for myself, you know. At least let me go to Nuklakayet with you next time, Papa."

Papa smiled. "I can just imagine what Mamma would say to that," he said.

So could Erinia. So she didn't say any more.

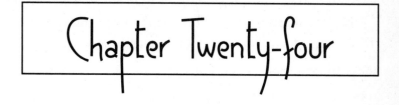

Chapter Twenty-four

ON A LATE GOLDEN SUMMER EVENING AFTER THAT LONG, cold winter was over, Erinia was trying to sleep.

There were mosquitoes in the room, so she crawled under the covers and pulled in all her toes and fingers and head so that nothing peeked out. She could hear them whining close to her head, but they couldn't bite her through a wool blanket. After a while it got hotter and hotter under there, and her own hot breath made her feel cross. She poked her head out of the blanket and took a deep breath of cool fresh air. Right away the soft wings of a mosquito brushed against her lips, so she pulled her head in again. She said one of the words in English that she wasn't supposed to say.

There were all sorts of mosquito bites. The worst ones were on a bone. Like on your eyebrow or on a knuckle.

No, the worst ones were between your fingers or toes. Those were the most terrible. Erinia wished there were no such thing as mosquitoes. But Dall had said that mosquitoes were very useful and that maybe there wouldn't be any birds if there weren't any mosquitoes.

But still.

Then she heard Papa calling from the yard. He wasn't just calling, he was yelling, which was something Papa never did. And Old Man Kozevnikoff was hollering for Lena as well.

Erinia bounded out of bed and pulled on her dress and ran to the kitchen, carrying her moccasins.

Mamma and Nilaat and Kate and Lena were in the kitchen, frozen in place, looking at one another with wide eyes. Papa was still calling to them.

"Edzegee!" said Mamma. I'm scared.

"No! Come!" said Erinia. "Papa sounds happy."

But when they opened the door, they saw all the people from the fish camp running into the store, looking over their shoulders as they ran, calling out in dismay, their faces horrified. When Mamma and Lena and Kate saw that, they dashed back into the kitchen and ran into the back rooms, looking as horrified as the others.

Erinia's heart began to thump in her chest, but she took

Nilaat's hand and together they stepped cautiously out into the yard.

Papa was in the wood yard, laughing, looking delighted. He grabbed Erinia and Nilaat by their hands and made them run down to the riverbank with him.

Then he pointed.

"Look!"

And there was a big white house moving right up the river toward them.

Something connected to the back of the house was turning around and around, flashing sparks of sunlight and river water as it moved. When the house gave out a horrible blat, Nilaat and Erinia screamed and hid their faces in Papa's shirt.

The house had a tall stovepipe coming out of the top of it, and there was black smoke billowing out from that stovepipe. There was a little porch going all around the house, and people were waving at them from the little porch.

Erinia drew in her breath sharply. Of course! This was the steamboat the telegraph men had talked about!

She smiled at Papa, and then she looked up to the odinochka to see if Mamma and Kate were looking out the window.

"A steamboat, Mamma," she yelled. "A steamboat!"

It looked beautiful in the golden late-night sun, like something in a dream. Papa didn't take his eyes off the steamboat. "They built boats like that in the shipyards at New Arkhangel. We boys used to go down and help rake the sawdust sometimes." Then he looked down at the girls. "When I was very young, they built a big sailing ship there. My father carried me in his arms to see it."

When the boat got closer, they could see that written on the side of the little house in fancy black letters was the word YUKON.

Erinia pointed out the writing. "Why is that written there, Papa?"

"Boats have names just like people," said Papa.

Erinia looked at Papa to see if he was joking, but he wasn't.

The *Yukon* was pushing two flat, low boats piled high with boxes and barrels.

When the steamboat pulled up to the bank in front of the store, the men on the steamboat laid out long boards from the boat to the top of the riverbank, and then they came across the bouncing boards to visit.

A tall, fair-haired man was the first across, and he came right up to Papa and Old Man Kozevnikoff.

"I'm Captain Raymond," he said. "United States Army." They shook hands all around, and Papa and Old Man Kozevnikoff said they were Ivan Kozevnikoff and Ivan Pavaloff. Then Papa introduced Mikhail and Stepan and Pitka to Captain Raymond.

"Why aren't you wearing your uniform?" Erinia asked suddenly.

Captain Raymond smiled at her. "You speak English very well. You must be Erinia."

Erinia smiled to say yes, but she wondered how the captain knew her name.

"Well, Erinia, we don't have very many men on this boat," he said. "I have to turn my hand to loading wood and other work, so I don't wear my uniform."

"The telegraph men said their uniforms were useless," said Erinia.

Captain Raymond laughed. "And they were right," he said. He cleared his throat and made himself look important.

"Miss Erinia, I have a package for you. From William Dall. When he heard about our trip, he said, 'You must give this to Erinia Pavaloff at the Nulato odinochka. She's a special friend of mine.'"

Erinia was too surprised to say anything.

"Dall?" asked Papa. "Is he still in the country?"

"Yes," said Captain Raymond. "He stayed after the telegraph crew left, and he's doing some collecting around Saint Michael for the museum."

"Oh!" said Erinia yearningly. "If only he would come and see us again."

"I'm sure he will, if he gets a chance," said Captain Raymond kindly. "I'll get the package for you right away.

But perhaps you all want to come aboard and look around?"

Pitka was nearly dancing with excitement, and he ran across the boards so fast that he almost fell off when they bent and bounced under his feet. Erinia and Nilaat laughed at him as he swung his arms wildly, trying to get his balance back.

Then it was their turn to walk across. Erinia suddenly remembered that she was still holding her moccasins, and she bent to put them on. Then she and Nilaat walked across the boards very slowly. They took little steps so the boards wouldn't bounce, but still they bent under the girls in a sickening way. Erinia didn't let out her breath till she got to the other side.

The captain showed them the little rooms inside the boat where the men slept, and a place where the men could play cards when they weren't working. He took them to see the furnace where they burned wood, which turned the water in a boiler into steam. Then he showed them the kitchen where they cooked and ate. The steamboat was like a little odinochka on the water, with everything imaginable someone would need.

"Would you like some coffee?" the captain asked, and though no one liked coffee, they didn't want to be rude, so they sat at the little table and drank it.

"How far upriver are you going?" asked Papa.

"Almost all the way to the headwaters," the captain

said. "The United States government has sent me to Fort Yukon to survey and see if the English trading post there is in English territory or if it's in American territory. If it is in Alaska, then of course they will have to leave."

The captain told Papa that the *Yukon* would need hundreds of cords of wood to keep the engine going. He asked Papa to tell everyone who came to Nulato that he would buy wood from anyone who would cut it.

Old Man Kozevnikoff went up to the store to call out the people who were hiding there. Some had hidden in the barracks, and some were crouched behind the stove. They were still half afraid when they came down the bank, but most of them came. Even Mamma and Lena and Kate came to stand on the bank and look, and Old Man Kozevnikoff was standing with them, waving his arms about. Erinia knew he was trying to get them to come on the boat too.

The captain and Papa stood on the little porch and laughed at the way the others edged away from the bank and clustered together for safety.

Erinia and Nilaat hung over the porch railing and called across to Mamma and Lena and Kate. They were very proud of themselves to have been so brave.

The steamboat's cook went across the gangplank and gave everyone from the fish camp a piece of hardtack from the big box he carried. The captain called out to invite them all to come on board, but only a few dared to do that.

"Kozevnikoff!" the captain called. "Tell them I want to buy fish, any fish caught today."

Old Man Kozevnikoff nodded and turned to tell everyone in Athabascan what the captain had said. Erinia saw some of the people shake their heads and make the sign for hutlaanee. Then Old Man Kozevnikoff called up, "They won't sell you any fish."

The captain looked unhappy when he turned to Papa. "Why won't they sell me fish?" he asked in a cross voice.

"They won't sell fresh fish to white men because white men don't treat the fish with respect," said Papa. "If anyone breaks the rules about throwing the bones away, they believe they won't catch any more fish."

The captain looked as if he would like to make a sharp answer, but he held his tongue.

"Well, can they sell me dried fish, then?"

"Oh, yes," said Papa.

The captain leaned over the railing again. "Dried fish, then," he called to Old Man Kozevnikoff.

Then the captain took them into the little house on top of the boat, where he showed them the big wheel that he used to steer the boat. There were big windows made of clear glass on three sides of that little house. You could see all around you, as if you were outdoors.

Pitka had poked around the boat with the same kind

of fierce curiosity he'd shown when the telegraph men showed him their things. Now he looked intently at all the instruments in the wheelhouse and asked a dozen questions. When the captain saw how interested he was, he said, "Would you consider going to Fort Yukon with us? I need a man to help with the boilers."

Pitka didn't even take a breath.

"Yes," he said. Then he threw Papa an asking look and Papa nodded slightly, though he looked a little taken aback. Erinia looked at Nilaat with dismay. Not her Pitka, too.

Then, while the boat took on wood, Pitka ran to the odinochka to get some things to take with him on the steamboat.

"Before I forget," said Captain Raymond. He bent and opened the door to a little storage space next to the big wheel. He took out a package and gave it to Erinia.

"It's a book," said Erinia joyfully, for she could feel that through the wrapping. A *fat* book.

They all watched while she opened it. It was by someone called Charles Dickens, and it was called *The Old Curiosity Shop*. Inside there was a letter from Dall.

"My dear Erinia," she read,

> "I was sure you must be tired of Uncle Tom's Cabin by now, and ready for another. I know you girls especially will like Little Nell in this book. I think of you and the others at

*the odinochka every day, and of the good times we had there.
And I hope when you read this book, you'll think of me."*

Erinia stared at the book. She was afraid she was going to cry. When she looked up, they all were smiling at her.

"Oh, Erinia," said Nilaat. "A new book to read. How wonderful."

And then, in no time at all, the steamboat was gone and Pitka was gone with it.

Mamma was stony faced. She'd known all along that one of the new things would take her sons, that nothing could hold them since they learned how wide the world was, and how many interesting things there were to see and do.

And that was the beginning of the steamboats and their new life.

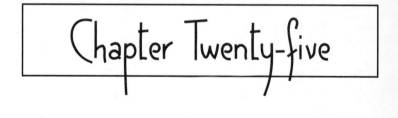

Chapter Twenty-five

THE NEXT YEAR TWO NEW STEAMBOATS, THE *Saint Michael* and the *New Racket*, as well as the *Yukon*, traveled up and down the river. They were much bigger and more beautiful than the *Yukon*, but Erinia always liked the *Yukon* best because it had been first.

Pitka came back to the odinochka only when his boat was taking on wood. In the winter he helped repair and paint his boat, which was pulled up on the beach at Saint Michael, getting it ready for the next summer. He married a part-Russian girl named Sarah, and that was another sister-in-law that Erinia and Kate had never seen.

Little log cabins sprang up outside the walls of the

odinochka, built by some men from up the Koyukuk River who came to stay in Nulato all summer so they could cut wood for the steamboats.

One of the steamboat captains had a whole set of Charles Dickens in his cabin, and every time he came to Nulato, he would loan Erinia another volume.

This captain also had a little dog with shining black eyes that was like no dog they'd ever seen. She had a beard and mustache and bristling stiff black hair. She ran excitedly about on her funny bowed legs and barked at everything. The captain showed Erinia and Nilaat the tricks his dog could do, and they were enchanted to see her sit on her rear end and put her little paws up like a squirrel.

On one boat there was a horse, standing quietly with his head down, pawing gently at the deck. It was just as Erinia had imagined when she was little. She *did* think it was a moose at first, just as she and Papa had joked. One of the deckhands ran to the bank to pick armfuls of fresh green grass for the horse, and while he fed him, Erinia and Nilaat ran their hands over the horse's smooth back and laughed to see his skin twitch and flinch under their fingers. He had very beautiful, sad eyes, and Erinia and Nilaat wished they could have him.

Another boat had a black man, a tall, strong man with skin as dark as a moose's and thick, crinkling hair. He was so tall he had to bend almost in half to shake their hands.

He smiled an enormous smile at the two girls. "Bet you never saw a black man before," he said.

Erinia knew she was staring, but she couldn't help it. She thought he looked just as she'd imagined Eliza's husband, George, in *Uncle Tom's Cabin*. It was as if they'd read the book so much that it had come to life.

"Were you a slave?" Erinia asked at last.

He shook his head a little. "No. I was raised up north," he said. "My mother, she was a slave." Then he straightened up and wiped the sweat off his brow with his forearm. "Those times are gone now," he said. He smiled his wonderful smile again and said, "You girls be good, and when we come back, I'll bring you some candy!"

Erinia and Nilaat watched for him every time that steamboat came, but he had gone to work in the mines, the captain said, and they never saw him again.

There were more and more people on the river. Most of the men on the boats were Americans, but there were men from every country in the world as well. They weren't explorers, as they used to be, but men looking for gold.

Besides the miners there were other men going upriver to start new trading posts to sell food and hardware to the prospectors.

A little Frenchman named Francis Mercier stopped in Nulato with his big freight boat to wait out a storm. He was the trader at Nuklakayet, and Papa and Old Man Kozevnikoff had known him for many years. Erinia loved to hear him talk, the way he bent the English words and made them sound better. And when he spoke French, she thought it was almost as sleek and flowing as Yuri's Spanish.

Mercier taught the men to play checkers. "Will you be *rouge ou noir?*" he'd say. The red or the black. Papa and Old Man Kozevnikoff were so pleased with this game that they played every chance they got. Mercier taught the girls to play as well, though Erinia was not much interested because when you'd finished a game of checkers, you had nothing to show for it. When you made bread, there were the loaves lined up on the table, sending a little steam into the air. And when you sewed or cut wood, you could sit back and look at the thing you'd done. She liked doing things that had a result.

A new American trader came to Nulato to start another store down where the new cabins were built. It would be a summer store, not for trading furs, but to sell groceries and supplies to the miners. His name was Roberts, and his helper was a part-Russian boy from the mouth of the river named Sergei Cherosky.

Papa and Old Man Kozevnikoff were not upset about this. They said there was plenty of business for everyone, and they even helped Roberts and Sergei build the store.

Roberts was a good-natured fellow and often came to the odinochka to drink tea. He liked to joke with the girls and told them that he was going to get them miners for husbands.

Old Man Kozevnikoff was very happy to have visitors so often, and sometimes when a boat had to stay overnight for repairs, the miners took out their instruments and sang and played in the evening while everyone danced. There was no telling what would happen when a steamboat stopped to take on wood, and Erinia felt like they were part of the world again.

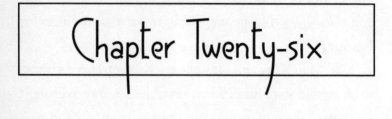

Chapter Twenty-six

THE YEAR THAT ERINIA AND NILAAT TURNED FIFTEEN, little skinny Nilaat suddenly became as round as a bear cub and heavier than Erinia. It made them all laugh to see her, remembering how she'd been when she came to them, all sharp bones and smile.

She wasn't as tall as Erinia, though. When they'd stopped growing, Erinia wasn't as tall as Kate, and Nilaat wasn't as tall as Erinia.

"My stair-step girls," Old Man Kozevnikoff called them. "Soon you'll have admirers," he said. "The boys will be asking for you girls, and Pavaloff and I will have to run them off!"

Now that she was full grown, the idea of admirers didn't upset Erinia the way it used to.

Kate already had a sweetheart, a young miner who'd come through on the *Yukon*, and when Sergei Cherosky came around, Erinia got a little silly. Nilaat teased her because even though Erinia didn't like to play checkers, she'd look happy to play when Sergei wanted a game. Nilaat, she liked everyone.

One cold day Papa was chopping the ice out of the water hole when the dogs began to bark their warning bark. He went to the bank, but he couldn't see very far, so he called to Mikhail to take a look.

Papa went back to the kitchen, where the women were all sewing. Lena was using a long string to measure Old Man Kozevnikoff for the harnesses for his new moose-hide mitts, and Erinia was very carefully cutting the moose hide. Papa opened the door so suddenly that she almost made a mistake.

"Runner coming," announced Papa. Old Man Kozevnikoff and Papa looked at each other, and Erinia thought, as she often did, how much those two could say to each other without speaking.

"Stepan and Mikhail are harnessing the dogs," said Papa. They would pick up the messenger to save him the last mile of his trip and bring him to the odinochka.

It wasn't very often anymore that a runner was sent with a message. In the old days young men who were strong and fast often went from camp to camp with messages that someone had died, or about the winter festival or something like that. They ran most of the way, and some of them were faster than the fastest dog team. Elia used to be such a strong runner, and Old Man Kozevnikoff had sometimes sent him with a message to the Koyukuk people.

Mamma jerked her chin at the girls to tell them to fold up their sewing. She got up and cleared the table and went to start the samovar so she could give the messenger tea. She had her mouth folded tight, so Erinia knew she was worried. They all knew it wasn't likely that a runner came with good news.

Stepan and Mikhail brought the sled right up the bank to the door of the store and came in with the messenger. The ruff on his parka was so heavily frosted that they couldn't see his face until he'd pulled his parka over his head.

"Demientieff's son, isn't it?" asked Old Man Kozevnikoff in a glad voice. The messenger nodded his head and held his hand out to Old Man Kozevnikoff to shake in the Russian way.

"Pavaloff," said Old Man Kozevnikoff, gesturing to Papa. "Stepan and Mikhail and my wife, Lena. And this is Pavaloff's family," he said, sweeping his hand toward Mamma and the girls.

"I knew this boy when he was just as high as my knee," said Old Man Kozevnikoff. He was so pleased to see the boy that he'd almost forgotten that the boy had some kind of message. Erinia forgot for a second too, thinking how very tall this boy was, with long legs like a crane, trying to imagine him as short as Old Man Kozevnikoff's knee.

"Sit down, sit down by the stove," said Old Man Kozevnikoff. They all watched the boy anxiously.

He seemed hesitant to start, so Mamma brought him a cup of tea, and Lena cut the loaf of sugar and pushed it toward him.

The boy swallowed, and the bone in his skinny throat moved up and down in an interesting way.

"Elia sent me," he said. Old Man Kozevnikoff's face turned hard. Erinia was afraid to hear what the boy would say next.

"Elia killed a man from the lower river, and he says to tell you that the relatives are going to come." Lena gave a little scream and covered her mouth with her hands.

"Who was this?" asked Old Man Kozevnikoff in a very quiet voice. He fumbled in his pocket for his pipe, as if the boy's answer wasn't important to him.

"Alexie Tachik, from Andriefsky," said the boy.

"I know that family," said Old Man Kozevnikoff, looking at the boy with surprise. "From when I worked at Andriefsky. The Tachiks are all good friends of mine. Is Elia sure they'll be coming for him?"

"He's sure," the boy said. "That's the sort of people they are, and they've talked about it to everyone."

That was the Indian way to revenge a death. Old Man Kozevnikoff took a long time to fill his pipe, and then he opened the stove to get a coal to light the tobacco. After he'd drawn on his pipe a few times to make the smoke come, he turned to the boy again.

"How did this happen?" asked Old Man Kozevnikoff.

"It was over a ball game. On the river. Tachik got angry when he lost the ball. You know how good at that game Elia is. Tachik lost his temper and hit Elia with a big spruce pole. And Elia took his knife to him before he could do it again. He died right away."

"Where is Elia?" asked Papa.

"He left Ikogmute right after it happened, and they're traveling here from Unalakleet. His wife is with him. He's coming here."

"I know those people," said Old Man Kozevnikoff in a puzzled way. "They wouldn't harm my family. They used to call me *Tata*. Papa. They said I was like a father to them."

No one said anything. Mikhail and Stepan went out to take care of the dogs, and Papa took the messenger to the kitchen so Mamma could feed him.

Erinia and Nilaat and Kate put their arms around Lena, who was crying softly. Old Man Kozevnikoff walked up and down the store, running his fingers through his white hair until it stood up in wild tufts.

Erinia had never seen him so upset.

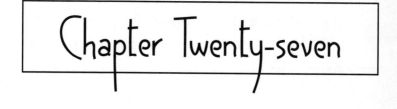

Chapter Twenty-seven

As soon as the Demientieff boy had told Old Man Kozevnikoff everything he knew, they sent him to the barracks to sleep. Then Papa turned to Mikhail and Stepan.

"Shut and bolt the gates," he said.

Old Man Kozevnikoff started to protest. "Surely that's not necessary," he said.

"Kozevnikoff," said Papa. "You think that nothing bad will come of this, that people will be reasonable."

Old Man Kozevnikoff spread his hands and shrugged his shoulders. "It's no sense imagining the worst," he said, though Erinia knew that a short time before he had been imagining the very worst himself.

"Yes," said Papa. "That's exactly what we must imagine. For Elia's sake."

Erinia had almost forgotten that the gates could be closed. The last time they'd been closed was when she was very young. The time the Kaiyuh people had come to trade and someone had come in terrified, reporting that there were Eskimos hiding in the woods.

At the time she'd thought it was a great adventure, and she was very pleased at all the excitement. Now she suddenly wished for her brothers. It didn't seem like there were enough of them at the odinochka to handle such terrible trouble. For the first time she realized that Stepan and Mikhail and Papa and Old Man Kozevnikoff were not young men.

Then Papa said all the men must take turns in the watchtower, the one that looked upriver, so that the Tachik relatives could not sneak up and surprise them.

"But Papa," Erinia said. "Your eyes are so bad. You and Old Man Kozevnikoff can hardly see any distance. Neither can Stepan." Papa blinked. She could see he'd forgotten that. "You'd better let us girls do the watching."

Papa looked shocked at that idea and so did Old Man Kozevnikoff. But before either of them could say anything, Mamma spoke up. "She's right, Ivan."

Papa and Old Man Kozevnikoff had to agree that sending watchers who couldn't watch was foolish, and that even though Mikhail had good eyes, he had too much work to do. So when it was daylight, Nilaat went to the watchtower in her heavy winter clothes. After an hour Erinia brought her a cup of tea.

They watched the messenger leave, and then she and Nilaat leaned on the window opening.

"You can see a long way from here," said Nilaat, "but every little movement makes your heart beat hard. I almost yelled, 'They're coming!' when a raven landed in the top of that spruce tree."

Erinia stayed in the tower and Nilaat went back to the house to warm up, and then in an hour Kate came to relieve Erinia.

While they were watching from the tower, Mikhail cleaned all the guns, and he hung one by each of the rifle holes, which had been cut long ago into the log walls of the store. He tried the plugs in those holes to be sure they came in and out easily. Stepan oiled the sliding bolts on the store door and fixed a padlock on all the other doors. They could use only the store door, which made a longer trip to bring in water and dump the slop buckets, but it was safer to have only one door that could be opened.

For the next few days Mamma and the girls didn't go into the woods to snare rabbits, and Erinia didn't go out to fill the water drums. Instead Stepan went to the water hole with Papa, and one of them always carried a gun.

They filled all the extra barrels and stored them in the house in case there came a time that they couldn't go outside the gates.

Lena, their boisterous and happy-go-lucky storyteller, who bustled about with the energy of a woman half her age, had come almost to a halt, and sometimes she just stopped what she was doing and sat. And often tears would fill her eyes.

Kate and Erinia and Nilaat tried to distract her. "Lena, show us how to knit the way the soldiers do!"

She'd offered to show them before, but only Nilaat had had the patience to practice the tedious knots over and over until they became second nature. But Lena just looked at them and smiled absently, making a little helpless gesture with her hand.

Erinia brought her the Aleutian basket she'd been weaving. "Show me again how to do the top of this," she asked. But Lena closed her eyes at that, puckering up her eyelids with pain.

"Oh, child," she said, "I can't think."

Mamma worked just like she always did, but she was grim and dogged and she never said a word. She wasn't talkative at the best of times, but Mamma utterly silent made everyone tense.

In between chores Papa and Old Man Kozevnikoff sat together in front of the stove, heads together, talking.

When Erinia brought them their breakfast, Old Man Kozevnikoff smiled and tried to joke with her, but she knew he was just pretending.

Kate was as good as could be and worked right along with Mamma, and you couldn't see that she was afraid, except that she didn't bother to carefully fix her hair, and instead wore braids like Nilaat's and Erinia's.

One afternoon Papa and Old Man Kozevnikoff began to make a pile of things in the middle of the store. Things for the trail: new snowshoes, and a good rifle, ammunition, warm clothes. They put together bales of dried fish and set them outside by the door, ready.

Kate and Nilaat and Erinia could tell by this that they were going to send Elia somewhere else when he came.

"Mamma, where is Elia going to go?" Erinia asked. But Mamma just shook her head. It was hutlaanee to talk about plans like that.

Erinia went to Papa. "Will Fedosia go with Elia?" she asked.

"Of course not," he said. "Elia will need to travel very fast."

These preparations put heart into Lena, and the next day she made a pair of beautiful, warm sealskin boots from the skins she'd had Mikhail get when he went to Saint Michael to trade with the Eskimos. She sewed without stopping from early morning until the boots were finished late at night. And then she brought out the huge pair of wool socks she'd made when the telegraph men were with them and had taught her to knit. She showed them to Erinia ruefully.

"Too big, you think?" she asked. "And look at these dropped stitches. I haven't got time to make a better pair."

They were really very large—Erinia thought she could have worn them on her arms up to her armpits— and certainly weren't as beautifully made as the ones the soldiers wore. But she said, "They were your first pair, you know," and Lena smiled at her.

Mamma made stacks of rusks from the new bread and set Nilaat to sewing tilth. She boiled a whole bag of beans and put them outdoors to freeze in little piles, the way the soldiers had done. That way they needed only to be heated in a skillet over the fire.

Then she and Kate patched Old Man Kozevnikoff's heaviest parka, which he hadn't worn for two winters.

"He won't need that again," said Lena. Old Man Kozevnikoff's hip had stiffened up so badly that he couldn't go on any long trips anymore. He walked with a little limp now, which made Erinia feel sad. Mamma put a new wolverine ruff on the old parka, and then they were finished with the outfit of beautiful, warm clothes for Elia.

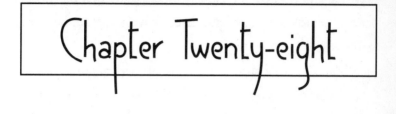

Chapter Twenty-eight

"I SEE THEM! I SEE THEM!" NILAAT SHOUTED DOWN FROM THE watchtower the next morning. "They're coming! Look, look!"

Erinia ran up to the tower, with Mikhail close behind her. Her heart was pounding so hard she could hear it in her ears. There were only two people coming, on snowshoes, and Mikhail was sure it was Elia and Fedosia.

Mikhail held his hand to his heart and took a deep breath. "I can't run up those stairs like I used to," he said.

Erinia was out of breath too, so she leaned against Mikhail's shoulder to rest a minute.

Mikhail went out with the dogsled to pick the two up, while the rest of them waited in the store. Lena's face was pale and she picked nervously at her apron. Nilaat sat by her side and rubbed her back. Mamma put water on to boil for the samovar and got out dried fish and bread, her face grim.

"Papa," Erinia said, "will the relatives be behind him?"

"We don't know, Erinia. The Demientieff boy seemed to think they'd be on their way soon, but who can tell? Sometimes people who are angry cool down in a few days. Maybe they'll give it up."

Stepan watched the sled pull up the bank, and then he opened the stockade gates and bolted them shut behind them. Mikhail stopped the team in front of the store, and Elia helped his wife out of the sled. They were both covered with frost, even their eyelashes. Their eyes weren't bright with excitement or crinkled in laughter like the eyes of the company men when they had come in the cold winter. Their eyes were tired and strained looking.

Lena and Old Man Kozevnikoff pulled the two inside. Old Man Kozevnikoff embraced Elia, and then he hugged Fedosia, too, frost and all.

"Son," cried Lena, "at last! Here you are safe at home. Oh, how we worried. How we worried!" Lena helped Fedosia pull the parka over her head, and Fedosia began immediately to cry.

She was a big-boned young woman with those clear green eyes Papa said you often saw in children with a blue-eyed Russian father and a dark-eyed Indian mother.

She was very tired from their long walk over the portage and very frightened. She fell into Lena's fat arms with a little scream and didn't leave off crying for an hour. Erinia thought about how Lena had imagined their first visit, with fat babies for her to play with. She'd even long ago made some little fur boots and a little hat for those imagined babies.

Elia's face was haggard, but he tried to laugh and joke the way he had in the old days.

"How long did it take you?" asked Papa as Elia sat on the bench, untying his boots.

"Only six days after we got to Unalakleet," he said. "It was a good trail."

"Are they behind you?" asked Old Man Kozevnikoff.

Elia looked at him for a minute. "I don't know," he said.

Mikhail and Stepan came in after seeing to the dogs. Nilaat and Erinia took Elia's and Fedosia's frosty outer clothing to the racks by the stove to dry. Mamma had the tea ready in the samovar, and Kate brought in the bread and lard and fish. Fedosia and Elia ate hungrily and drank a lot of tea. Fedosia pressed up against Lena as if all the safety in the world lay in Lena's plump body.

Erinia knew everyone wanted to ask questions, but they were waiting until Elia and Fedosia had finished eating.

Elia had become thicker through the chest and the

arms, his jaw wider, and there was a serious look about him when he was quiet. Not a boy anymore.

"Oh, my little Erinia," he said when she brought him more tea. "You're a grown woman now, and I'm sure you've forgotten me!" She put her arms around him to show him that she hadn't.

"I heard you have a new sister," he said. He pulled Nilaat's apron strings teasingly and smiled in almost in his old way.

He had heard all of the odinochka news already. He had heard about Minook and Pitka getting married and about the deaths in the Kaiyuh band. He'd heard about the last trip Papa and Old Man Kozevnikoff had taken to Nuklakayet. Erinia smiled to remember the way the telegraph men had always been amazed at the fast way news traveled up and down the river and out to the Kaiyuh and back.

When Kate came in with more sugar, Elia teased her about her Russian ways, and he praised Lena's good salt fish and Mamma's bread, as he'd always done. But Erinia could see that he didn't really feel like smiling. Where was the lighthearted Elia, the tall, handsome boy with never a worry in the world?

Erinia felt sad when she saw the way Elia kept running his hand through his hair until it stood on end, just the way Old Man Kozevnikoff did.

Papa cleared his throat, and Erinia knew that meant

he was going to ask Elia questions. Mamma stood up, and Erinia knew she didn't want to hear about the trouble.

She nodded her head at Lena, so Lena said, "Come, Fedosia. You two can stay in Nilaat's room, and Nilaat will move into Erinia's room."

All the women went into the kitchen, but Erinia stayed. She was sure they'd try to send her away, and if they did, she'd say, "I want to know what's happening. I can't help if I don't know what's happening." Papa looked at her hard, but when she folded her lips together hard like Mamma, he looked away.

She filled their cups from the samovar, and Old Man Kozevnikoff said, "Tell us what happened."

Then Elia told them about the games on the river and the fight. He told this with his face unmoving and his voice calm, but when Papa asked about the man he'd killed, Elia's face grew angry.

"He was a troublemaker in his own village and every-where he went. He was big and he'd been pushing people around all his life. Everyone was afraid of him. Lazy, too. I'm not sorry Alexie Tachik is dead."

"What made you think his relatives would come after you?"

"I didn't think it at first. But as soon as he was dead, all the people there told me, 'You've got to leave. When they hear about this, his brothers will kill you.' They live in

Andriefsky, you know, and Alexie was just in Ikogmute for the potlatch. They said his brothers were just as mean as he was, and I guess that's true."

In a troubled way Old Man Kozevnikoff said, "I knew their father, Kantilnuk, and their grandfather, too. They were good people. Good friends of mine."

"That was a long time ago, Papa," said Elia, "and they are all dead now."

They were quiet for a minute, and then Elia said, "Do you think I was foolish to leave?"

"No, no," said Old Man Kozevnikoff. "You did the right thing. It's hard to know how people will behave."

But Erinia knew that Old Man Kozevnikoff just couldn't bring himself to believe that his old friend's children would demand the old kind of justice.

Mikhail and Stepan began to talk quietly about other killings and other relatives who had taken revenge. Erinia was sure they were doing it to make Old Man Kozevnikoff see how dangerous the situation was. Papa told Elia about a whole family that had packed up and left and gone over the trails to Fort Yukon to get away from the relatives after their son had killed a man.

Sometimes the family killed a relative of the person who had done the murder. Sometimes they killed the murderer himself. There were other stories about bargains that had been made, a sort of payment for the murdered person, and in one case, when a woman had been killed, the killer's family gave the victim's relatives their oldest daughter to replace the woman who had been killed. Different people handled such things in different ways, and the differences had grown greater since the Russians had come into their country.

Erinia filled their cups again and again. Papa sent her to get them some tobacco, and soon the smoke from the pipes filled the room and swirled around in the draft from the door.

"Ivan and I have made a plan," said Old Man Kozevnikoff. "You know my old friend Kokrines, upriver." Kokrines was the last Russian on the river, the only one on the Yukon who hadn't gone back to Russia when Russian America was sold to the United States. He had a trading post near the mouth of the Novi River, and a lot of people lived there year-round to be near the store. Papa and Old Man Kozevnikoff always stopped to see him when they went to Nuklakayet, and so had the telegraph men. Kokrines was far enough away for safety. Old Man Kozevnikoff was sure the Indians from the mouth wouldn't go so far into the territory of the Tanana Indians.

"He'll keep you there. There are lots of people living there by his store, too. They would help you," Old Man Kozevnikoff reassured Elia. "Just get out of the way for a while. Just to make me happy, go to Kokrines and stay a few months. Just in case. You can come back when the ice is gone in the spring."

Papa said, "Fedosia can stay here with us. I think she's about played out. And she would slow you down."

Elia looked at Stepan and Mikhail. They nodded at him. "It's a good idea, Elia," said Stepan. Elia looked down at the table.

"Yes," he said. "I'll go to Kokrines."

Then he looked at his father. "They might come here."

"It's a long way," said Papa.

"It depends on how mad they are," said Elia.

Stepan said, "They're not going to come where there's a stockade and so many people to deal with. The Kaiyuh people will be here soon, and the woodcutters from the Koyukuk will be back before long. And Roberts and Sergei will be here after breakup to open their store again."

"You're probably right," said Elia.

So the next day they sent Elia off with enough food for a week's journey, with a sturdy sled and two of their biggest and fastest dogs.

Old Man Kozevnikoff sent presents for Kokrines—a beautiful pair of wolf mittens Lena had made, tea, tobacco, a fine Russian beaver hat, and one of the army blankets.

They stood on the bank to watch him go upriver until they couldn't see him anymore, and then they went inside.

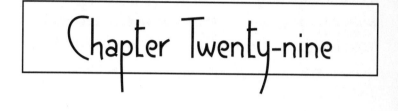

Chapter Twenty-nine

FOR TWO WEEKS AFTER ELIA LEFT, THE GIRLS KEPT WATCH and the gates were always carefully locked. Erinia's heart gave a terrible thump every time the dogs barked, and everyone else was jumpy too. They heard nothing of Elia, but they didn't expect to, since no one would be going upriver until the spring thaw. They were sure he'd reached Kokrines safely.

But it was impossible to keep up such a pitch of readiness for long. The company men came with the spring supplies and trade goods, the Kaiyuh people came to trade, and everyone was so busy they stopped thinking about Tachik's relatives. The gates were left open again, and no one looked out from the watchtowers.

And too, there were many more people living around the odinochka than there had been in the dead of winter when Elia had come through. Roberts and Sergei returned to get ready for the summer trade, and the Koyukuk River men came to cut wood for the steamboats. More people made Erinia and the others feel safe.

Lena and Mamma were pleased with Fedosia because she sewed so well. Fedosia's Athabascan was Ingalik, the language the Indians spoke far downriver. No one at the odinochka could understand Ingalik without a lot of trouble, so they all spoke Russian together.

Fedosia talked to them about her mother, who had died just after she and Elia were married. Her mother's other children had died when they were small, and so Fedosia was a treasured child. She cried and cried with her hands over her face when she talked about her mother. Erinia was sure that was why Fedosia had clung to Lena since she'd first come.

"Was your mother fat?" she asked Fedosia.

"Oh, yes," Fedosia said, smiling at the memory. "Just like Lena."

She told stories about her village near Ikogmute and the way her people lived. They didn't travel all the time like the Kaiyuh people, and they had a special big house just for dancing and ceremonies. Her father was a Russian, but he'd died when she was little. She didn't mind that he was dead, because he'd been mean. Erinia was very glad that Fedosia had Elia to look after her now, because she hadn't had a very good life.

Mamma tried to teach Fedosia to make the good black Russian bread, but though she could sew beautifully, Fedosia's bread was somehow not as good as Mamma's.

In the spring when the river ice broke up and began to move down the river, all the men left Nulato to go into the hills to hunt caribou: the Koyukuk woodcutters, Mikhail and Stepan, and even Roberts and Sergei. It had been a very hungry spring and they needed meat. Old Man Kozevnikoff couldn't go because of his bad hip, and Papa had been very sick for a week with a fever and terrible cramps that had doubled him over. So Papa and Old Man Kozevnikoff were the only men left behind.

That was when the relatives came.

The women were in the kitchen sewing when a shadow passed the window and blocked the light, and then the kitchen door swung open and six men with rifles filed into the kitchen. Mamma and Lena, Fedosia, Kate, and Nilaat didn't move. Their needles paused in their sewing, they stared at the men and said nothing. Erinia stood to face them so fast that she knocked over her chair.

"Where's Kozevnikoff?" the tallest one asked in

Russian in a very pleasant way. Erinia knew who these men were, and she didn't trust her voice, so she didn't answer.

"Where's Kozevnikoff?" the man asked again.

"Sit down," Erinia said, pointing to the chairs. "I'll get him."

She made herself move slowly and calmly. Her hands had begun to sweat, so she wiped them on her apron and went toward Mamma and Papa's room. The tall man nodded to the five other relatives, and they went back out the kitchen door.

The man followed Erinia, but she pretended she didn't notice. Old Man Kozevnikoff was sitting by the bed where Papa was lying. He looked up when Erinia and the man came into the room.

"Kozevnikoff," said the man in a hearty voice, very friendly.

Old Man Kozevnikoff got up and shook the man by the hand, looking anxiously into his eyes. The man was as tall as he was.

"My brothers and I came across the pass. We're staying down at the winter houses."

Old Man Kozevnikoff still looked searchingly at him, but the man was smiling in such a friendly way that Erinia could see Old Man Kozevnikoff relax.

"Please come to us," the relative said.

"Yes," said Old Man Kozevnikoff. "I'll come. We'll talk. Yes." The tall man turned and left the room and went back through the kitchen.

Papa started to get out of bed, but Erinia stopped him. "Lie down, Papa, lie down!" she said.

Papa held out his hand imploringly. "Ivan, you mustn't do this," he said.

Papa almost never called Old Man Kozevnikoff by his first name. "Don't worry, Vanya," Old Man Kozevnikoff said soothingly. "You see how friendly he was. They'll want something, of course. I'll pay them what they want. We'll settle this like old friends."

Erinia could see from his face that he really wasn't worried. He had such faith in friendship, Old Man Kozevnikoff.

He smiled at Papa and patted the blankets in the way you'd comfort a child. Then he turned and left the room.

Old Man Kozevnikoff had been gone for hours when the women in the kitchen heard someone slamming at the padlock on the store door, trying to break it off. Erinia threw a wild glance at the others and dashed out of the kitchen door before they could stop her. When she got to the store door, she saw that the smallest of the relatives was hitting the big iron padlock with the butt of his gun. The other relatives were standing around him, waiting for the padlock to give.

"Stop that!" shouted Erinia. They didn't look at her, and the little one kept chopping at the padlock as if she weren't there. His gun butt splintered and he gave a curse. The others laughed at him.

"Where is Kozevnikoff?" she demanded.

"Dead," the tall one said. Then he turned his face to her—his cold, expressionless face, that face that had smiled so pleasantly at Old Man Kozevnikoff. Erinia felt such hatred for him that she was faint with it.

The six men all looked at her in the same way, their eyes glittering in the noon sun, their faces cruel. Erinia knew then that the relatives were going to kill all the rest of them.

"Leave the padlock alone," she said angrily. Her voice was shaking. "What do you want in there?"

"Tobacco," said the tall one.

"I'll get the key," she snapped.

The tall one motioned for the little man to stop chopping at the padlock, which was much too big and strong to be broken with a rifle butt.

Erinia walked slowly around the store to the kitchen door.

Dead, dead, he was dead. *We are all going to be dead*, she said over and over in her head.

When she opened the door, she could see that Lena and Fedosia had been crying and Mamma was shaking violently. *Oh, Mamma,* thought Erinia, *to have to go through such a terrible thing again.*

In a bossy, strident voice that didn't even sound like hers Erinia said, "Fedosia, you're the strongest. You and Nilaat go get Papa and take him to the storage shed." She snatched up a set of keys by the door. "Now! Just put him on a blanket and carry him that way. He can't walk. And you stay there in the storage shed. Kate, you take Mamma and Lena and go to the shed too. I'll lock you in."

The women still didn't move, so Erinia screamed at them, "Do what I say! Now! Now! They're going to kill you!" Lena's face was stricken, and Erinia saw that she knew that her husband was dead.

"Hurry! Do you want to die?" Fedosia and Nilaat came stumbling out of Papa's room, nearly losing him out of the blanket. Papa was very white.

"Erinia," he said as they carried him past her, "get away from them!"

Erinia ran ahead of them to the storage shed. The others followed her, their feet punching through the rotten snow. Lena fell heavily and the jagged shards of melting snow cut her arm. When she got up, Erinia saw that blood was dripping fast onto her apron. Erinia opened the storage shed lock, and when they all were in, she slammed the door behind them. No time to fix Lena's arm, no time for water or food or anything else. No time to get them warm clothes. She locked the padlock, and then she thrust the key down in the melting snow by the door. She buried all the other keys down there as well and kept only the key to the store padlock. If the relatives didn't see the keys maybe they wouldn't think of taking the things in the other storage sheds, maybe they wouldn't find her family.

She ran back to the store, where the relatives were still standing, waiting.

"I'll get the tobacco for you," she said. She fumbled with the padlock, and as she started to open it she looked up. Six rifles were pointing at her chest. She could see herself thrown up against the door by the force of the bullets, see the blood that would spatter on the old worn boards of the door. Her teeth clenched so hard that her face jerked, as if she had a chill.

Her hatred for these men was so fierce she knew she could easily kill them and wished she had a gun to do it. She unlocked the padlock. Two of the relatives kicked on the door and it swung in with a *screak*.

The store was cold, and Erinia could suddenly see how Old Man Kozevnikoff had looked standing there by the stove, his pipe in his hand, warming himself. "Where are my girls!" he'd bellow. She felt a stab of grief so sharp that she nearly cried out.

The short one took the big padlock from the hasp. "Give me the key," he ordered. Erinia jerked the key away from him and he hit her clenched fist with the rifle butt. The key fell out of her hand and he bent with a sneer to pick it up.

If she kept defying them, they were going to kill her for sure. And then they'd find the others and kill them too. Or maybe they'd never find them and they'd die in the storage shed, starved and cold. But she couldn't stop herself, couldn't keep her fury from making her half crazy.

As the relatives swept around the store grabbing anything in reach from the shelves, Erinia suddenly picked up a piece of wood from the woodpile and threw it at the relative who was sweeping rifle shells off the shelf and into his bag. He swung around and pointed his rifle at her. "Murderers and thieves," Erinia screamed. "The store doesn't belong to Kozevnikoff, it belongs to the Alaska Commercial Company at Saint Michael. You've done enough damage today. You've killed a good man who was like a father to everyone, just because his son killed one of you.

"If you kill me and the rest, there'll be war. My brother Minook is married to the medicine man's daughter at Nuklakayet, and he'll send his tribe down to kill you. And the soldiers from Saint Michael will come and wipe you out and your whole family."

The tall one said something in Ingalik that made all the others stop what they were doing to look at him sullenly. They began to talk to one another in their own language, which Erinia could not understand very well. Then they started to put some of the things they'd taken back on the counter.

"You go get Kozevnikoff," ordered Erinia. "You bring him to us, since there are none of our men here to bring him in. You cowards who make war on women, everyone will talk about you when they hear of this, how you hid away and waited till the men were gone."

Two of the relatives went up the trail and brought Old Man Kozevnikoff back down to the odinochka. He was sitting up in the sled with a smile on his face.

Erinia cried until the tears blinded her and her nose was running. She mopped her face with her apron, saying, "He's not dead. See, he's smiling. He's not dead. He's not dead."

She pointed to the store, and two of the relatives tried to lift Old Man Kozevnikoff out of the sled. But he was too heavy for them, and they called out to the others to help. Even with four of them they staggered under his weight.

"Put him on the table," Erinia whispered. Before they laid him down, she saw that he had been shot in the back.

The relatives had what they wanted, but still they sat around the store, talking and arguing. Erinia hunkered down against the wall and watched them. The hand the relative had hit with the rifle butt was swollen to twice its size. Broken. It hadn't hurt at first, but it had begun to throb horribly. But she wouldn't let them have the pleasure of knowing that they'd hurt her.

"Make tea!" one of the men said to her.

Before she knew what she was going to do, Erinia spit at him. He grabbed his gun off the floor and pushed the barrel against her throat. "Stop it," the tall one said. The other lowered his rifle and the men began to argue some more.

Many hours later, when it was almost midnight and the sky had darkened as much as it does at that time of year, the relatives suddenly got up and walked out the door, without looking at Erinia or Old Man Kozevnikoff. They went off up the trail, toward the winter houses.

Erinia got to her feet. Her legs and body were stiff and sore, and her hand hurt terribly. She walked slowly to the storage shed. The snow had melted so much in the time she was gone that she could see the top of the key showing above the snow. She opened the lock, and then, with her back against the shed wall, she slid down into a squat. She put her forearm over her eyes and said over and over, "He's not dead, he's smiling."

Chapter Thirty

Lena and Fedosia, Kate and Nilaat and Erinia sat up all night by Papa's bed, grieving for Old Man Kozevnikoff and terrified that the relatives would come back for them. In the morning Papa sent Erinia to see if the ice on the river had thinned out.

"There's some left, Papa, but it's not too bad."

"Then we must leave now," said Papa. "We don't know where the relatives are. We don't know if they've had enough revenge. We have to go to Saint Michael now."

Clumsy with fear, they wrapped Old Man Kozevnikoff in a canvas tent and dragged his body into the big freight boat. After they'd hurriedly gathered enough food and warm clothes for the trip, Erinia tethered their three dogs in the bow, while Kate scribbled a note to leave in the kitchen for Mikhail and Stepan to tell them what had happened.

They traveled silently. Lena and Fedosia had stopped weeping, but every time Mamma slept, she woke crying out. Her dreams were terrifying.

They had to stop every so often to camp on the banks and wait for the ice to thin out some more, so it took them more than a week to get to Saint Michael. Papa got better on the way and was almost well by the time they reached there.

At Saint Michael, Mamma and Lena washed Old Man Kozevnikoff and dressed him in new clothes from the company store. The village men and Pitka, who had been at Saint Michael all winter with his boat, helped Papa build a coffin, and they buried Old Man Kozevnikoff in the graveyard by the Russian church.

Mamma made a little fire by his grave and burned tobacco for him in the Indian way.

Stepan and Mikhail said that as soon as they had come back from hunting, they'd known immediately that something was wrong. No smoke, no barking dogs. Then they'd seen that the store door was open, and they saw the blood on the table by the stove. When they found the note, they put their canoes in the water and came to

Saint Michael, traveling four days in the cold spring rain with no rest. But they were too late to help bury him.

Erinia had finished with crying until she saw Mikhail and Stepan, bareheaded in the rain, kneeling by the grave, sobbing with frustration and anger because they hadn't been there to protect him. Then she began again and went to her bed aching with grief.

Stepan and Mikhail said everyone had left Nulato, gone back to their homes, for fear of the relatives. Roberts had closed up his store, and he and Sergei were on their way to Saint Michael too. There were wild rumors about raids in every camp on the Yukon. Old Man Kozevnikoff's murder filled everyone with terror.

They slept for a time in the company barracks, but after a while they found other places to stay: a little cabin for Mikhail and Stepan, and a smaller one next to the church for Mamma and Papa. Erinia and Kate and Nilaat stayed in a larger house by the fort with Lena and Fedosia.

Minook came to Saint Michael when he heard about the murder. He'd stopped at the odinochka and had brought the precious samovar and some other things he thought they'd like to have with them—the sewing kits and the men's pipes and the blueberries Mamma had put away in birch-bark baskets.

Elia came a few weeks later. He sat by his father's grave

for hours, whispering, "It's my fault. It's my fault." Erinia and Papa had to pull Elia away and take him back to the house. "Elia," said Papa. "You know that Ivan would a thousand times rather that he was the one taken and not you." But that didn't comfort Elia, whose guilt was too deep for comfort.

They all took what work they could find. Lena cooked at the fort, and Fedosia and Nilaat scrubbed clothes in the fort's steaming laundry rooms. Papa and Mikhail and Stepan worked for the company in the warehouses and at the docks. Kate and Erinia made money sewing boots and mittens and fur hats for the soldiers and the miners who were going upriver to look for gold.

Erinia couldn't stop thinking about that terrible day. What had happened to Old Man Kozevnikoff in the time he was with the relatives? What had they said to him? Did he finally know that old friendships meant nothing to those men? Did he know they were going to kill him?

She took these questions to Papa, but Papa had turned inside himself somehow. He only shook his head and didn't answer. He'd become very gray, and stooped when he walked.

And poor Mamma, worn out by her terrible dreams, died in the early winter.

It was many years before Papa would ever talk with Erinia about the old days in the odinochka. He said that remembering good times made your heart ache when you knew they'd never happen again.

But Erinia was glad for her memories, and she told her children how it was when the Kaiyuh people came to trade, the way Old Man Kozevnikoff bellowed, "Nyet, nyet," about Lev's legs kicking out like the pistons on a steam engine when he did the Cossack dance. And how Papa put her to sleep with stories of New Arkhangel. She told them about sliding on the beaver skins and playing with the trade buttons, and the stories Mamma told her about the starving times and about how she and Nilaat had backed away from the bear. And about the time the telegraph men made taffy for them, and how they'd danced in the summer dust to Yuri's fiddle.

And how they'd danced.

Author's Note

When I was a girl growing up in Fairbanks, Alaska, everyone knew who Erinia Pavaloff was, though there weren't very many who knew that was her name. Everyone called her Grandma Callahan. She lived a few houses down from my stepfather's mother, who was her niece.

Sometime around 1936 Grandma Callahan hand-wrote a little five-page memoir of her life, probably for Judge James Wickersham, who was doing research at that time for his book *Old Yukon*. Not only didn't he include her story in that book, but the memoir was lost and only found years later when a sorter at the Salvation Army in Seattle, Washington, was going through a box of papers

Erinia Pavaloff Cherosky Callahan, ca. 1890
(Collection of Geraldine Lizotte)

before burning them. More than thirty years after Grandma Callahan's death my stepsister, Johanna Harper, Erinia's great-great-niece, sent me a copy of the memoir, which had been printed in the *Alaska Journal*. And that was how I first learned that Grandma Callahan's name was Erinia and that she'd been right in the middle of practically everything that was going on at that amazing time in Alaskan history.

I'd always wanted to write about those years on the Yukon, and Erinia's story seemed like a good way to do it. I wanted my book to be an accurate, absolutely real portrayal of the times and place and people.

I soon found, to my dismay, that it was impossible to be accurate or absolutely real, or even reasonably certain of having written the truth, because there was so little information.

Erinia wrote five pages, period, and most of that was about the murder of Ivan Kozevnikoff. The explorers wrote journals, but there were endless, maddening contradictions about dates or events or people.

So how much of the book is real? All the characters in the book except Nilaat, Stepan, and Mikhail were real people who lived in the odinochka or visited during Erinia's childhood. (There were a dozen more fascinating people I could have included, but there just wasn't room in the story.) Erinia didn't tell what the people at the odinochka were like, except that she called Kozevnikoff "a jolly old man." Frederick Whymper and William Dall said little about the people in Nulato, and the only Pavaloff child they mentioned was Pitka. Since there was no way of knowing what the people were like, I made everyone nice, just because that's the kind of world I'd prefer, given my choice, and when you write a book, you have that choice. I doubt very much if they were all as nice as I've written them. And I can only imagine how Erinia and the other characters would have reacted to the people who came to Nulato and to the things that happened.

The events are real, but I left out twice as many as I put in. Nulato has too much history for just one book! Sometimes, for the sake of the story, I changed the date something happened.

The murder scenes are taken right from Erinia's memoirs. Other people told the story differently but she was, after all, the only one who was there.

This is what happened to the people in the story after the murder, according to Erinia's memoir:

The family stayed in Saint Michael for a year, except Papa, who worked for the company at Andriefsky. Mamma died, and Erinia married Sergei Cherosky when she turned sixteen. Then they all went back to Nulato, where Papa ran the store for a year, and after that they all went to Eagle, following the miners.

Erinia Pavaloff Cherosky Callahan, ca. 1920
(Collection of Geraldine Lizotte)

Minook and Pitka and Erinia and their families lived and worked up and down the Yukon, often together. They worked as interpreters for the many trading posts— at one time they worked for the Frenchman, Francis Mercier—and they prospected as well. Cherosky and Pitka found gold near Circle City but lost all their claims to the white men, who said they couldn't file because they weren't citizens, as they were part Indian. Minook was the first to find gold near Rampart, but he lost those claims as well. In 1904 Minook went to court and asked to be made an American citizen. The judge ruled that Minook was already a citizen according to the provisions of the purchase from Russia. But of course by that time someone else had already mined the gold Minook and Pitka and Cherosky had found.

Kate married a prospector named Sonniksen at Old Station, near what's Tanana today, and moved to California. She had two sons. Sergei and Erinia had four children, but only two, Helen and Axinia, lived past childhood.

Pitka and Sarah were the parents of eight children, one of whom was my children's great-grandmother, Lena Pitka Milligan Chute.

My stepfather's mother, Louise Minook Harper, was one of Minook and Liza's sixteen children.

And all the children had children, and grandchildren

and great-grandchildren, and now the family is huge. (My sister has a family tree that was put together by Alice and Hazel Knox, nieces of Erinia's, showing the descendants of Marina and Ivan Pavaloff. If we stretch it out, it reaches seventy feet.)

Sergei died in 1902, and in 1904 Erinia married Dan Callahan, who was a member of the Alaska House of Representatives, and they adopted a little boy, Dan. When Erinia and Callahan divorced, she supported her children with her sewing. Erinia and her daughter Helen raised Lee Alder, one of Axinia's granddaughters. Erinia died in 1955, when she was either ninety-one or ninety-five, depending on which records you believe.

There is no mention anywhere of what happened to Lena, or Elia and Fedosia. Apparently Elia and Fedosia had no children, but Elia's brother, Ivan, did, and so there are a lot of Kozevnikoffs around today. According to their family records, Ivan Kozevnikoff Sr. was not a creole, as he is in my story, but was born in Russia.

In 1888 a Catholic church was built at Nulato, and in 1891, the first school. For a short time there was even a hospital in Nulato. In 1898 Father Jules Jetté began his study of the Athabascan Koyukon language and wrote all he could learn about the customs of the people. Without his work, knowledge of the old Athabascan ways would now be lost.

Captain Raymond did find that Fort Yukon was in American country, so the English Hudson's Bay Company had to leave Fort Yukon and move across the border to Canada to do business. Dall went on to be a world-famous scientist. Whymper's book *Travel and Adventure in the Territory of Alaska*, with its many drawings, was published in 1868.

Telegraph lines were finally in use by 1901, and in 1911 the telegraph was replaced by the wireless. Now every Alaskan village has telephones. Steamboats went up and down the river until 1952, when they were replaced by boats with big diesel engines, which still deliver the freight to all the villages.

Alaska is still a huge, empty country when you fly over it. The villages along the Yukon are as tiny as they always were, and people travel to them mostly on the river or by airplane.

The music learned from the miners is so popular there's an Athabascan fiddling festival every year in Fairbanks. No one speaks Russian anymore, but many people all over Alaska have Russian names, are baptized Russian Orthodox, and drink lots of tea.

In many villages in Alaska people are bilingual, and in one village in which I lived the old people spoke five languages and learned English from the radio.

The Russian Orthodox Church supported seventeen

schools and two orphanages for nearly fifty years after the purchase, since it was many years before the U.S. government provided schools or hospitals.

And it was nearly sixty years after the purchase before all the native people could vote.

Sources

Adams, George R. *Life on the Yukon, 1865–1867*.
Kingston, Ontario, Canada: Limestone Press, 1982.

Callahan, Erinia Pavaloff Cherosky. "A Yukon
Autobiography." *Alaska Journal* 5 (1975): 127–28.

Dall, William H. *Alaska and Its Resources*. Boston: Lee and
Shepherd, 1870.

Grauman, Melody Webb. *Yukon Frontiers*. Fairbanks,
Alaska: Anthropology and Historic Preservation,
Cooperative Park Studies Unit, University of Alaska,
1977.

Jetté, Jules, and Eliza Jones. *Koyukon Athabaskan Dictionary*.

Fairbanks, Alaska: Alaska Native Language Center, University of Alaska, 2000.

Loyens, William J. "The Changing Culture of the Nulato Koyukon Indians." Doctoral thesis, University of Wisconsin, 1967.

McQuesten, Leroy N. *Recollections of Leroy N. McQuesten of Life in the Yukon, 1871–1885.* Dawson City, Canada: Yukon Order of Pioneers, 1952.

Netsvetov, Iakov. *The Journals of Iakov Netsvetov.* Vol. 2, *The Yukon Years, 1845–1863.* Translated by Lydia Black. Kingston, Canada: Limestone Press, 1980.

Tikhmenev, P. A. *A History of the Russian-American Company.* Translated and edited by Richard A. Pierce and Alton S. Donnelly. Seattle: University of Washington Press, 1978.

Whymper, Frederick. *Travel and Adventure in the Territory of Alaska.* New York: Harper and Brothers, 1869.

Wickersham, James. *Old Yukon.* Washington, D.C.: Washington Law Book Company, 1938.

Zagoskin, Lavrentii A. *Lieutenant Zagoskin's Travels in Russian America, 1842–1844.* Edited by Henry N. Michael. Toronto: University of Toronto Press, 1967.

Acknowledgments

The following people generously provided me with
documents, stories, pictures, and memories:
Mark Freshwaters, Gabe Nollner, Elaine and
Todd Kozevnikoff, Mary Warren, Geraldine Lizotte,
and Lee Alder. And many thanks to Judy Redmond,
who read the manuscript.